THE CEDAR TREE

HEATHER REYBURN

Cover design: Lana Pecherczyk.

ISBN 978-0-6451234-0-1 Print Edition

Heather Reyburn

www.heatherreyburn.com

For Hilary, my friend.
Dreams really do come true!

CHAPTER 1

*G*race Campbell released her grip just enough to prevent fingernails from cutting into her skin, as rural Queensland, its heat haze distorting the horizon, enveloped her thoughts. The LandCruiser lumbered over the rattly old stock grid, skewed sideways, and hit a huge pothole.

"Shit."

Grace wrestled with the steering wheel, glancing briefly in the rear-vision mirror. The vehicle swung back onto the track and she crossed her fingers, hoping Daniel hadn't overheard. Determined to set a good example for her three-year-old son, she tried hard not to swear, but sometimes her mouth just erupted before her brain engaged.

Obliterated by dust, the horse float swayed dangerously behind her. She gripped the wheel tightly, her heart pounding in her chest, took a deep breath, and focused on the track ahead. Her load contained nothing particularly valuable—just boxes of what she believed would help her cope with her new life in the bush. But still, she didn't want it strewn across the paddock.

Gently, she rubbed her aching shoulder. This morning's predawn incident added to her heartache and anxiety, and the knot in her stomach tightened while bile burned the back of her throat.

Thick dust blanketed the truck travelling behind them, concealing the driver. Pete slowed and changed gears as he prepared to follow her over the grid. No doubt in total control, perched comfortably in the driver's seat, she could just picture the satisfied smile spread across his face. He much preferred the responsibility of their precious horses and kelpie dogs to their son. The piping chatter of kids drove him nuts, and if he was honest, she was sure he would admit he really hadn't wanted to be a father.

In the LandCruiser, Grace's apprehension, anxiety, and just a little bit of excitement added to her already churning stomach. Pete's confidence in acquiring this new job was award-winning, but Grace had her doubts.

She heaved a sigh. *What on earth am I doing? Did Pete's charm and smooth talk bluff the agent into recommending him for this job?*

"Are we there yet?"

Grace grinned in the rear-vision mirror at her son, roughly awoken by the grid crossing—his introduction to Tullagulla.

"Yes, sweetie-pie. We're here. Keep a lookout for the house."

Daniel leaned forward as much as his harness would allow, his eyes lit up with anticipation and excitement. Never one to miss the action, Min, Grace's black and tan kelpie dog, raised her head from the floor beneath Daniel's feet.

As the runt of the litter, Grace had named her Mini Mouse, shortened to Min. She was proving to be a handy little dog around both sheep and cattle; her big heart defied her slight build.

However, her loyalty to Grace and Daniel infuriated Pete. The other dogs, Molly and Tweed, lived in kennels and were kept tied up except for their daily run or when working. Little Min was different, special, and had been Grace and Daniel's constant companion.

Bumping down the track over ant nests and potholes, Grace's heart sank as she absorbed the ravages of drought. Except for a few gnarly old gum trees and scraggly gidgee bush, she observed nothing but dust, dry saltbush, and a property that oozed neglect.

A large dam wall appeared on her left, raising the question of water availability—the most precious of commodities. Memories of growing up on a green and rolling property on the upper reaches of the Clarence River overwhelmed her. Water certainly wasn't a problem there—she was used to good rainfall and beautiful scenery, not to mention the love and support of her family. So far, it looked as though Tullagulla was going to fall a long way short of that.

C'mon, girl. Buck up, she chided herself. *You're thirty-one, fit, healthy, and about to start a whole new life.* Inhaling deeply, she eased off the accelerator, forced a smile on her face, and swallowed, her mouth as dry as sawdust.

"I see it." The shrill voice jogged Grace from her reverie. Glancing in the rear-vision mirror, she followed Daniel's gaze. A chimney.

As the vehicle swept around a clump of brigalow, Grace's eyebrows rose another notch. A brick chimney and grey roof were just visible through a high scrappy hedge. Straight ahead, on the other side of an open and dusty intersection of tracks heading every which way, a long low shed squatted in the dirt. It was old and propped up at each corner with huge round timber logs resembling rigid soldiers on sentry duty. A rambling bougainvillea threatened to gobble one end of the shed, its bright magenta bracts a dramatic contrast to the brown and dusty surrounds.

The tracks divided and Grace braked hard, her thoughts a tangled web. A glimpse of yards, stables, and a woolshed were away to her left. Immediately to her right was a new corrugated iron vehicle shed complete with two silver roller doors, and she squinted at the reflection of the bright afternoon sun. Towering over the back of the shed, a windmill clanked lazily in the otherwise still and silent paddock. In the corner of the homestead yard stood a huge red cedar tree.

"Wow, that's beautiful." Grace breathed her surprise. The tree's filtered shade consumed both the lawn and a semicircle of paddock. Beyond the tree, the paddock sloped away to the east, a limp windsock suggesting an airstrip and dusty road beyond.

Grace allowed the vehicle to creep forward again, pulling on the handbrake as they halted outside the fence. Switching off the engine, she sat in silence and gazed at the homestead.

Above the gate leading into the yard, an overgrown and tumbling honeysuckle vine grew, precariously supported by an equally rickety and rusted archway. A brittle attempt had been made at a garden below it, and Grace marvelled at the strength and determination of the surviving vegetation. A single red rose lifted her spirits a notch, the straggling bush almost devoid of leaves.

"Mum. Let me out."

Grace released her seat belt and opened the door before helping Daniel. She breathed in the warm, dry air as the truck shuddered to a halt in the middle of the crossroad behind them. Air brakes screeched and hissed and the engine quietened. Thankful that her sunglasses concealed the trepidation in her eyes, her heart still leapt as Pete jumped down from the cab.

His commanding presence, his height, and his hopeless good looks turned heads, including Grace's. Those bright blue eyes crinkled around the edges when he smiled and his black closely trimmed beard outlined straight white teeth that belied his love of sweets and all things unhealthy. She had first set eyes on him at a campdraft competition five years ago, and Grace still pinched herself at the realisation that she was Pete's wife. After knocking her off her feet with his charm, and in a whirlwind of steamy romance, they'd progressed rapidly from long phone calls to driving hundreds of kilometres to meet for weekends—mostly at campdrafts, rodeos, or polocrosse carnivals. Within a year, she had been pregnant with Daniel and they were married.

Now Pete strode towards her, his mouth twitching as he chewed a toffee. A short, stocky, middle-aged man appeared from the track behind the machinery shed. Limping slightly, his face was partially hidden by a huge black Akubra hat. He was almost upon them when Grace swivelled, hiding her surprise at his eye patch.

A wide, beaming smile welcomed her. "You'd be the new fellas then?" he drawled as if time was never of the essence.

Grace waited.

"Yep! Pete Campbell." Pete shook the older man's hand, nodding towards Grace as he swallowed the remainder of his toffee. "My wife, Grace, and my son, Daniel."

Grace smiled her acknowledgement. "Hi."

"Greg Walton. Two IC here at Tullagulla. Welcome. Been here a while now, so anything ya need to know, just ask." He nodded towards the homestead and looked at Grace. "Me missus has been in and lit the stove for ya and put some fresh food in the cold room. Squire killed a mutton—it's hangin' in the slaughter-house. Will cut it up and bring it over later."

"Thanks, Greg." Grace returned his friendly smile.

"We'd better get these horses and dogs unloaded. Are there pens somewhere for them?" Pete interrupted.

"Sure, I'll take you down to the yards and stables and show ya round."

"So, what happened to your eye?" blurted Pete.

Grace cringed at her husband's lack of empathy but Greg just laughed.

"Stupid accident. Workin' in the shed and threw a screwdriver up onto the trailer as I bent down. I wasn't watching and the bastard bounced back at me and the sharp end went fair into me eye. You wouldn't believe it, would'ya?"

Pete roared with laughter. "Bet you don't throw things around now, hey?"

Grace flinched. *What must this poor guy think?* Most people who heard that story would show a bit of sympathy, but not her Pete.

If it bothered Greg, he didn't show it.

They really do breed them tough out here, she thought ruefully.

"Nah, take life a bit steadier now." Greg laughed. Glancing in Grace's direction, he waved his arm at the homestead, turned, and ambled unevenly towards the truck, calling back as he went. "Go in the house and have a gander, and I'll show the boss the lay of the land."

Pete gave an approving nod as he spun on his heel and caught up.

The truck started again, Pete's head turned away from them, dismissing all but his companion.

"Come on, mate," Grace called to Daniel as she pushed the gate open. *Who's Squire?*

The drooping honeysuckle tried to wrap around her head and tickled her arms as she ducked underneath it. Careful where she put her feet, she led Daniel by the hand as they negotiated the cracked concrete pathway. Where the path reached the house, there was a wide stone step, so old that a groove was worn in its middle.

Reaching to push open the screen door, Grace glanced up at the high, rapidly moving wispy clouds strewn across the sky, indicating strong winds above. A flock of screeching cockatoos flew overhead. She turned, stepped through the open door onto the gauzed-in veranda and faced a second door leading straight into the kitchen.

A sudden gust of wind charged the windmill into action and Grace jumped. The blades turned, clanking loudly, stopping again as fast as they had started. After kicking off her boots, she helped Daniel remove his before entering. They stood still, taking in the new surroundings.

Dominating the room was a large table—solid, scrubbed, and surrounded by eight chairs of different styles, colours, and conditions. Behind it, the long bench held a sink in the centre, a small gas cooktop in the corner, and wooden under-bench cupboards all the way along the wall. There was no sign of a dishwasher or any modern conveniences except for the cooktop, a relic of the 1970s with its three gas rings. The old Aga, spilling warmth into the already hot room, stood on the wall next to the pantry door, and a comfy-looking couch squatted beside the wood stove, transporting Grace to a previous time in history. Memories of a neighbour's farmhouse from her childhood flashed through her mind. Painted red and white with an old grey benchtop, this kitchen had a cosy 1960s retro appearance, just as her neighbours had. Shoved hard against the window overlooking the entry gate was a small, polished wooden table supporting a surprisingly new television.

Well, at least the place looks clean. Grace gave a small sigh of relief.

Holding Daniel's hand, she explored farther. On the left wall of the kitchen were two doors. The first revealed a small room containing a single bed, a book-case, and an old timber wardrobe. The cook's room. A flutter of anticipation mixed with a few drops of dread coursed through Grace. *Yikes, I am now the cook.*

"Can I play in here, Mum?" Daniel piped up. Leaning on the bed, his little forefinger traced the patterns in the faded but beautiful old patchwork quilt.

"Sure. When we unpack the car, we'll put your toys in here and it can be the play room." Grace smiled indulgently at her young son.

Behind the second door was the farm office. An

ancient leather-topped desk dominated the room and on it sat a new computer—as if to defy the aging process and introduce the mix of old and new. To the side were two shelving units laden with books, papers, and a myriad of old shoeboxes, yellowing and wearing various thicknesses of dust.

What will Pete think? Somehow I think it will be me who uses this room. She knew only too well how much he disliked office work, relying heavily on Grace's patience, practical knowledge, and good record-keeping skills.

Cautiously, she turned the handle on the corner door leading to the rest of the house. As it swung away from her, the kitchen flooded with bright sunlight. A wide corridor appeared to lead to the main house and was lined from floor to ceiling with glass-louvered windows along its left-hand side.

Grace stood, her expression resembling that of a stunned mullet as she began to grasp the enormity of the housekeeping job that lay ahead. There was a small room tacked on to the corridor containing a toilet and hand basin, and next to it, a modern refrigeration unit was linked to the corridor with a heavy, sliding insulated door. A fleeting image from the far doorway startled Grace. The hairs on the back of her neck stood on end and she froze, her pulse thumping so hard she was sure it would deafen Daniel. *Someone is watching.*

Whipping around, she almost tripped over her little boy in her attempt to flee. Sweeping him into her arms, she reached back to slam the door behind her, willing herself to take a second peek first. Puzzled and confused, there was nothing. She was sure she had seen a person standing at the end of the hall, but now, there was no one.

Bolting back through the kitchen, Grace pushed the screen door open to the outside air before casting a glance skywards as she regained control of herself.

"How weird?" She gulped deeply and her pulse attempted to return to normal.

A thunderhead was building in the west, a stillness in the air suggesting an impending storm.

Grace gazed around. The cedar tree, a shaggy plumbago hedge lining the east fence line, and a bit of green lawn to the side of the house appeared to be the only evidence of the property having had any love or water for a long time. Her tiredness now forgotten, her pulse slowly returned to normal as she convinced herself firmly that it had been a long day, and her imagination had been swayed by the age of the homestead. Dismissing her concerns, she squeezed Daniel's hand.

"Come on, mate. Let's go and have another look around."

CHAPTER 2

Two Weeks Earlier

Grace drove to the Brisbane airport to collect Pete, puzzled at his brief text demanding she pick him up well before his designated block of shifts should have finished. Her stomach churned with apprehension. Having to leave work in a hurry, she phoned her parents' at home to check they could care for Daniel a little longer today.

She loved her role as rural financial advisor at the local bank and working only three days a week allowed more time to be at home with Daniel. When Grace and Pete had married, Grace's parents had suggested they live in the empty cottage on their farm: her home. With the alternatives either being stuck in a rented house in Grafton or on the outskirts of Moura while Pete worked long days and weeks, it was a no-brainer. Pete's job in the central Queensland coal mine as a fly-in, fly-out dragline driver was not exactly family friendly.

However, it was good money and he liked working with other men, so if he was happy, she was too.

Both Grace's brothers were long gone from the home farm. Brendan farmed nearby with his bubbly, animal-loving wife, Leah, while Hamish and his wife, Kate, lived the fast-paced lives of professional solicitors in Sydney. Their two young daughters, entrenched in their expensive private school, were mostly cared for by their housekeeper-come-nanny, a practical Irish girl desperate to gain residency in Australia. As a result, the family rarely saw them, much to her parents' disappointment. Instead, they poured their love and attention into Daniel and each other. Grace marvelled at their teamwork and prayed that she and Pete would one day be the same.

Sitting in the passenger seat while Pete manoeuvred the LandCruiser in and out of the chaotic traffic, Grace's concern deepened as his mood deteriorated and his erratic driving increased. Her usual joyful anticipation faded rapidly as they cruised down the Pacific Highway towards the farm. They usually enjoyed a long and animated catch up, passing time quickly. This trip was different and the knot inside Grace tightened. Pete turned the music up to a deafening pitch for most of the journey, adjusting it as they veered off the highway towards their quiet rural road and announcing, "The mine's undergoing a restructure and I've been laid off."

Frozen with shock, Grace just stared at him. "So, what will you do?"

"Dunno. I've already rung the other mines and it looks like they're all cutting back. No jobs there either."

While Pete unpacked, the air and his mood darkened. Grace plodded over to her parents' house to collect Daniel, her head down, her heart racing. As she approached the house gate, her dad, Martin, bent over to feed his old dog—a chunky, devoted blue heeler called Banjo.

"Hi, Dad." He looked up, smiling and opened his mouth to respond as the back door flew open, revealing her Mum—a tad dishevelled in jeans and a bright pink shirt, her sleeves rolled to just below her elbow. Margot smiled indulgently at her daughter, holding Daniel's backpack, her gentle face flushed as Daniel ducked under her arm. "We've been playing footy in the hall."

Daniel giggled at his grandmother's admission.

Grace grinned at them both, remembering the number of times she and her brothers had been in trouble for playing football down the hallway. "How time and age changes things, ay, Mum?"

Margot laughed, the wrinkles around her eyes spreading out past the frames of her glasses as she tucked a stray greying hair behind her ear.

"Oh, well. I'm older and wiser now and I know how short life can be. There's plenty of things more important than preventing the odd scuff mark on a wall." She bent to give Daniel a hug, her smile radiant as she looked at her daughter and grandson.

"Very true."

Margot shot Grace a worried glance. "Is something wrong?"

Grace twisted her mouth. There wasn't much she could hide from her mum. "Pete's lost his job."

Her parents glanced at each other before her Dad responded. "Well, there are worse things that can happen in life, love. He's pretty handy so it won't take long for him to find another one."

Grace was grateful for Martin's reassurance, even if her mind was invaded by questions and doubts.

Carrying Daniel's backpack, Grace faked a happy smile when they turned to wave goodbye, while her thoughts returned to Pete. She wished he would open up to her and share his feelings and thoughts.

"Isn't the old saying, *A problem shared is a problem halved?* Why does he have to keep everything to himself?" She spoke aloud as they walked across the paddock to their cottage, Daniel running ahead and Min trotting faithfully at his side.

As Pete's drinking escalated over the week that followed, his communication barely progressed from a grunt to something more civil. With nerves as taut as a banjo string, Grace crept about the house as if on egg shells, afraid to say anything that might provoke him and make matters worse. Internally, she wrestled with rage and despair, her love for him tearing her emotions to bits.

Appearing at the laundry door with an overnight bag in his hand, she started as he announced, "I'll be away for a coupla days."

"Oh, okay?" Grace bit her lip. She considered questioning him further but it would only inflame his anger and she was rapidly learning what happened when she did that.

He turned and walked to the vehicle shed. Grace's heart pounded. As the LandCruiser roared down the road, anger replaced her nausea and she muttered sarcastically under her breath. "No worries, mate. Just take my car and leave us depending totally on Mum and Dad."

Pete had been well paid by the mining company, but somehow there wasn't much to show for it. He settled the credit card bill and not much else. He didn't even own a vehicle. Grace had bought her LandCruiser and horse float before she met Pete and kept her own bank account with her savings squirrelled away. But that certainly wasn't going to keep the family going for long. Her parents had given them the truck as a wedding present, perfect for taking the horses to competitions but not exactly convenient for grocery shopping.

For two days, Grace heard nothing. Not even a response to the texts she sent Pete each night. The loving goodnight texts Grace sent him while he worked in the mines, with a brief outline of hers and Daniel's days, had been the same. His responses had begun reasonably well, but over time, had dropped to just an emoji—if she was lucky.

Her stomach fluttered again, sending her running to the bathroom and preventing any desire for food. She gritted her teeth and scrubbed ferociously at the windows before tackling the floors. Anything to keep herself busy. Daniel scooted up and down the veranda on his trike, loading and unloading his toys into the back tray and keeping up a constant volley of chatter— sometimes addressing his toys, sometimes Min, and occasionally, Grace.

She flopped onto the top step, picked up her mobile phone and punched in her best friend's number.

"Hi, Gracie. I was wondering when you would remember me," Georgie joked.

"Sorry, Georgie. Things have been a bit . . . you know, awful." Her lip quivered and Grace blinked back the tears, glad Georgie couldn't see her.

"Oh, okay." Serious now, Grace could tell Georgie was listening. She imagined her friend collapsing into the squishy white couch, ignoring the glorious view of the ocean from her immaculate town house and drinking a mug of coffee as she commanded, "Spill the beans."

Grace poured her heart out, confident that Georgie was the one person with whom she could share some of the secrets only best friends can.

Grace and Georgie had started primary school together and been friends ever since. But while Grace's childhood had been spent on the farm mucking around with her two brothers and her pony, Georgie's was in a massive home overlooking the ocean in northern New South Wales, supported by her ophthalmologist dad and her mum who worked as a practice nurse in a skin cancer clinic—a world of difference for the girls.

"I'm here for you any time you get a chance to talk, Gracie. If you can't ring, just send me a text and I'll call you back."

They chatted for a few more minutes, Georgie's easy manner lifting Grace's spirits as they discussed Daniel, Grace's job at the bank, and the local gossip. By the time Grace hung up, her shoulders had eased somewhat, even if Georgie's concern had not.

Avoiding her parents' questions and worried looks, Grace kept herself busy, frantically cleaning, working in town while Daniel stayed with her mum or taking Daniel for a ride on Jarrah, her quiet little stock horse mare. With his helmet buckled tightly under his chin, his hands clutched the monkey grip at the front of her saddle as they walked sedately around the paddock, while Min trotted alongside them. When her mum called suggesting she and Daniel join them for dinner, Grace declined, making the excuse that she wanted a couple of early nights while Pete was off looking at better options for them all.

The rumbling diesel engine of the LandCruiser grew louder and Grace dropped her book and jumped to her feet, sick with relief. Her legs shook as her glance at the clock confirmed it was nearly midnight.

Pete threw open the door, his face alight with excitement, oblivious to the anxiety his departure and lack of communication had caused. "Meet the new manager of Tullagulla Station."

Grace reached out and hugged him, almost crippled with relief as she thought carefully before responding. "Where's that? Are we included?"

"Of course. It's an old property in Queensland and the homestead is big. I'll need you to be the house-keeper and back up for me."

"How far away?"

"Western Darling Downs. It'll probably take us a day or two to get there with the truck and horse float. Haven't seen it yet but I met the agent in Goondiwindi and he showed me photos and gave me the lowdown. We start in two weeks so you'd better hand in your notice tomorrow and start packing."

Grace stared at him as her mind processed the information. "What happened to the previous manager?"

"He died." Pete shrugged, annoyance creeping into his tone as his excitement deflated. Stepping towards her, his mood changed and his anger flared. "What's your problem? You're never happy, are you? Here I am, trying to do the right thing for my family, and you show no appreciation at all," he spat.

"Of course I'm happy. I'm really pleased for us all. I'm just taking a minute for it to sink in." Reaching out, she hugged him again, commanding her hands to stop shaking as she buried her face in his shoulder. "Come to bed now. It's late. Let's talk more tomorrow." she whispered.

Seemingly appeased, at least temporarily, Pete spun her around and pushed her towards the bedroom.

CHAPTER 3

A whirly wind blew across the yard, catching a loose sheet of iron on the shed. Grace jumped, jolted by the banging and flapping of the tin.

"Maybe we will bring good luck and good rain," she whispered, crossing her fingers as she spoke. It was April and it had been a long, hot summer with little rainfall. Out here, the years of drought had bitten hard, and the country was filled with skinny stock and desperate, depressed farmers.

Dragging herself and her thoughts to the Land-Cruiser, she hauled out the garbage bags filled with linen and clothes lying across the back seat, followed by the suitcases, boxes and esky from the rear section. Lining them up against the vehicle, she half watched Daniel playing with a pile of stones in the dust by the gate.

"Yoo-hoo. Welcome to Tullagulla."

She squinted towards the cheery call as she struggled through the honeysuckle carrying a box of toys and books. The box slipped in her hands, bashing her shins as it fell. Bending to re-grip it, she shook her head, silently chastising herself for being so nervy.

A short, plump woman stood next to Daniel clutching a casserole dish, a red-checked tea towel folded across its lid. Her round weather-beaten face and twinkly eyes were bright and welcoming, and Grace relaxed slightly as she rubbed her bruised shins. Wearing an old cotton dress and sneakers, the woman's grey wispy hair blew around her head like an unruly cloud.

"Gidday, luv. You must be Grace? And this little bloke's Daniel? Here's some dinner for youse all. I didn't think you'd feel up to cooking after ya big drive today."

"Oh, that's really kind of you. Thanks!" Grace grinned, taken aback by surprise and gratitude. The thought of having to operate that old wood stove, or the gas one for that matter, had made her feel sick. She waited for the woman to introduce herself, but she had turned to Daniel and launched into a one-sided conversation, still clutching the casserole. Daniel was listening intently, his startled look relaxing to a wide smile as he warmed to her.

After plonking the toy box on the ground, Grace reached out. "Would you like me to take that?"

Looking up, the owner of the kindly face suddenly seemed to remember why she was here and handed over the casserole. "I'm Beth—Greg's wife." She laughed like a schoolgirl. "We live in the cottage down the track behind the machinery shed." She rattled on, "Got two nice girls, both grown up and gone now, so I can help out any time with this little bloke if you need me?"

As she gazed lovingly at Daniel, Grace nodded, smiling, recognising a soul who needed to be needed. "Thanks for the offer. We've had a long day and I need to unpack, but perhaps we could have a cuppa together tomorrow and talk some more?"

Beth grinned again and went back to her conversation with Daniel.

Deep in thought as she trekked back and forth to the kitchen, Grace continued unloading the car, dumping the boxes and bags on the floor. Her heart was lighter; the knot in her stomach started to unravel.

Waving and calling hooroo, Beth strolled back towards her cottage and Grace bent down to Daniel.

"Come on. I'll give you a piggy-back and we'll go and see where Dad and Greg went."

They trotted along the track towards the woolshed, Grace snorting and pretending to buck like a horse, Daniel bouncing and giggling as he hung on around her neck and shoulders. Min galloped along beside them, leaping and frisking while her loving gaze remained glued to her owner.

"Let's see where the horses and dogs are."

She wanted Min to live up at the house with them and hoped that Pete wouldn't lose his temper again. They had already had a row over a dog's place. Her anger welled as the memory flooded back, her pulse pumping in her neck. She would never forget the incident, the first in their relationship, the unfathomable shock still as clear as crystal.

Standing up to Pete had resulted in a hard shove against the fence post, crashing her onto the barbed wire. Even when the blood continued oozing through her shirt and the handkerchief was wrapped tightly over the arm wound, he'd refused to apologise. She had driven herself to the doctor to have it stitched.

Straightening her back, Grace slowed to a walk, gently prising Daniel's grip from her sore shoulder and setting him beside her. Wincing, she drew a deep breath, shortened her stride, and slowed to Daniel's pace, silently vowing she would make the most of this adventure.

The sun faded, its orange glow drooping to the horizon as the few clouds darkened and the hope of a shower became a possibility. Grace breathed in the smell of dust and mulga, reviving memories of her field trips to the west when she was studying her agricultural degree, and her strength blossomed.

Sitting on the old stone step, she studied Daniel building little heaps in the dirt outside the gate once more while they waited for Pete's return. Normally a practical and sensible person, Grace's nerves twitched at the thought of going back inside the house alone. Inventing silent excuses, she daydreamed as the sun set on her first night at Tullagulla.

CHAPTER 4

Grace summoned enough courage to turn on the kitchen light and warm Beth's casserole in the microwave. Daniel was dusty and tired but, reluctant to leave the kitchen-end of the house, she sat him on the edge of the laundry tub in the little room to the side of the steps. Grace laughed as he squealed when his bare bottom touched the cold concrete of the ancient sink, and they chatted as she gave him a good wash.

After wrapping him in a towel, Grace opened the screen door for him. "Okay, mate, you go and find your pyjamas while I rinse out the tub."

"I found my jarmies," Daniel yelled as Grace entered the kitchen a minute later. He had indeed located his night attire and the contents of the suitcase were now spread across the floor.

While he dressed himself, Grace shoved the clothes

back into the bag and stood it against the wall in the tiny cook's room.

"Come on. Let's have some of this lovely dinner Beth's made for us."

She extracted a loaf of bread from the esky and dropped two slices into the shiny but well-used toaster on the pantry shelf. Ladling a good spoonful of the steaming hotpot onto the toast, her mouth watered.

It had been hours since she had eaten. She'd wait for Pete to come in first though, so they could open the bottle of wine she'd brought with them and celebrate their first night in their new home.

Lying next to Daniel on the narrow bed, Grace read stories to him as the breeze blew gently through the bedroom window, assisted by the erratic whooshing of the kitchen fan.

She woke with a start as Pete called out. Daniel was fast asleep beside her.

"Where are you, Grace?"

"Shhh. You'll wake Daniel." She could smell the grog on his breath. "Had a beer or two with Greg did you?"

Pete smiled. "Yeah, nice fella. We just cracked a couple to celebrate our arrival. I'm starving. What's for dinner?"

Grace bit her tongue. She should have just opened the bottle of wine herself and eaten alone. She very much doubted he would have even noticed. "Casserole," she replied. "On toast."

"Good."

As Grace buttered the toast and ladled the casserole

onto the plates, the delicious aroma reminded her how hungry she was, and they both went back for second helpings. The wine remained unopened.

The morning sun was high in the sky and she was on her third attempt at lighting the wood stove when the gate slammed.

"Mummy, Beff's here." Daniel's miniature trucks whizzed across the kitchen floor, their operator lying on his stomach. Min lay along the step, her head on her front paws as she watched Daniel adoringly.

Sitting back on her haunches, Grace called out. "Come in, Beth. Perfect timing. I think I need a lesson with this damn stove."

Beth chuckled as she pushed the screen door open and stepped over the dog, trucks, and three-year-old boy. "Let me show you, love. It won't give you no trouble once you know how."

Grace scrutinised intently as Beth gave her step-by-step instructions.

"Build up the criss-cross layers of paper, twigs, and small pieces of wood. Now twist a piece of newspaper into a tight twill, light one end, and gently push it into the firebox, touching the scrunched-up newspaper under the twigs. Then blow on the flames like this." She blew gently and firmly on the flame and sat back as the firebox leapt into an orange glow, growing and spreading rapidly.

Grace stared at Beth, her jaw slack with awe.

"Now, you need to watch it for a few minutes and feed it carefully, one piece of wood at a time, 'til it builds up and starts to throw out heat. Next time you go to town, you could buy a box of fire-lighters as well." They both giggled. Fire-lighters, although considered the cheat's way of lighting a fire, would have been a simple substitute to the paper twills and fiddling about. Beth struggled to her feet and dusted her hands together.

"You're amazing." Grace reached out and gave the older woman a spontaneous hug. "Thanks heaps. I think you might have to teach me a few things. Your dinner was delicious last night."

Beth laughed, shrugging shyly, clearly unused to compliments. "Had a few years of practice. You'll be every bit as good, if not better, in no time."

Grace's confidence and gratitude towards this warm and comfortable woman skyrocketed as she turned to the sink and filled the kettle. "Cuppa?"

"Ooh, yes please. Never say no to a cuppa, love." Beth looked at Daniel, smiling. "How's me little mate this morning?"

Beth plonked herself down in one of the kitchen chairs, and Daniel's face lit up as he carried his trucks over to her and piled them in her lap.

"I'm not very good with vehicles," Beth lied. "You had better tell me what each of these is."

Grace smiled as she busied herself getting out mugs and tea things while she waited for the kettle to boil.

Daniel chatted to Beth with such increasing confidence, a random observer would have assumed she was his adored grandmother.

Grace had to wait for Daniel to finish his spiel before she could get a word in edgeways. "I'm sorry, Beth. I've only got shop-bought biscuits to offer you. I'm not much of a cook when it comes to cakes and biscuits."

Beth's measured stare locked with Grace's green eyes and anxious face. "I can teach you, love. Perhaps we can do a deal? I've been trying to keep this house clean for more than thirty years now and I admit, I'm starting to find it a bit tough as me old knees give me gip. I know I'm not doing a very good job anymore. If you're able to do the cleaning, I could do the baking for us both. At least until you get the hang of it? I do love cooking," Beth admitted ruefully.

"Really?" Grace was delighted with the offer. "It's a deal. So, when we finish our tea, would you mind taking me through the house and explaining what you do and where everything is kept?"

"Of course, love. First stop, the laundry outside, then we'll start here and work through the house."

"Oh, we don't need to see the laundry. We've already checked that out. It was good to find the washing machine."

Initially disappointed to find only old double concrete tubs in the laundry, Grace had investigated further, uncovering what seemed to be a large box just inside the door with an old moth-eaten tablecloth. Her hopes had risen as a large, brand new automatic washing machine had been revealed.

As Beth's tour of the house and her explanation of her routine evolved, so did Grace's spirits. *Why on earth did I get the collywobbles yesterday when I thought someone was watching me? I must have been more tired than I thought.*

Grace hugged Beth once more. The older woman giggled shyly, touched by Grace's gratitude and turned the handle to the final door off the huge lounge.

Grace had peeped in earlier, but with the heavy drapes partially closed, the room was dark and her eyes had not adjusted before she was summoned by Daniel. As they stepped into the room now, she blinked, slowly adapting to the poor light. Her breath whistled through her teeth.

"Wow, this is massive."

"Sure is. This is the master suite. It hasn't been used since we've been here. Jock refused to live in any of this part of the house except the main bathroom. He slept in the little room off the kitchen, but he always insisted that the main house be kept spick and span just in case the owner ever turned up."

"And did he?" Grace asked.

"Not in my day. The last time Mr Lansdowne Snr visited, as far as I know, was just after he bought the place. I think he was a real townie and only purchased Tullagulla as a tax dodge. But just in case, I come in once a week and give the bathroom a quick wipe over, flick the duster around, and air the room. I don't keep sheets on the bed but leave the quilt on so it looks nice, and those old sheets are covering the armchairs to keep the dust off them. There's no television in the lounge, as you probably noticed. That little one out in the kitchen was Jock's. I think he bought it with his own money."

"So how did you manage to get the satellite dishes put on the roof?" Grace was curious.

"Oh, for some reason, they just turned up." Tapping the side of her nose she continued, "Just between you and me, I think the agent might have given Mr Lansdowne a tune up and made him realise he'd never keep staff if he wasn't prepared to give us a few comforts. We got the television satellite dish, the new washing machines, and then, not long before poor Jock died, we even got the internet dish. Still not much mobile phone reception out here, but the landline works okay and I've never used a mobile phone anyway, so nothing lost there." She giggled again.

"Have you met the new owner?" Grace was interested to know more about their illusive boss.

"No, never. But then again, I s'pose he only took over a coupla months ago. Apparently his father, Mr Lansdowne Snr, bought this place after Angus McLeod died, and that was back in the seventies. I've no idea how old this new bloke is, but the agent said he's an accountant so he probably won't have a clue about farming. There hasn't been a woman live in this house for as long as anyone can remember, so we're not too sure what the future will hold for us now." A frisson of anxiety crept into Beth's voice as she shrugged and Grace digested the information.

In an attempt to reassure her, Grace emphasised the positives. "Well, let's hope he's a really nice fella who wants to pour money into it and make it the best property around. You would think that if he had wanted to sell it, we wouldn't have been offered this job, right?"

Accepting Grace's logical explanation, Beth grinned again, taking Daniel by the hand as they turned to head back to the kitchen. "At least we have the two-way radio. It's been a lifeline over the years. The base is here in the office, but we have one in our house, the single men's quarters, machinery shed, and in each of the farm vehicles. Just need to be a bit careful what you say, cause there's lots of nosey parkers around the district and everyone can listen in. If they didn't quite hear what you said, they are just as likely to make it up."

Grace raised her eyebrows. She had already heard the two-way beep and crackle a number of times and although voices had boomed out to the kitchen, she'd struggled to understand what they were saying. So far, the only bit she had been able to make out was that most people said 'over' or 'out' before the next person spoke, just like in the old war movies she used to watch with her dad. "Okay, I think I might need a lesson or two on the use of that as well." She laughed.

"You'll be right, love. You kids learn much quicker than us old chooks. Right now, I'm going home to do some baking for youse. I'll pop over this afternoon with it and that husband of yours will soon believe his wife is the greatest baker Tullagulla's ever seen." She roared with laughter as she bent to give Daniel a cuddle. Turning back to Grace, she patted her on the shoulder, oblivious to the flash of pain momentarily crossing Grace's face.

"Ooh it's so nice to have another woman here." Beth's warmth moved Grace and tears pricked her eyes. A comrade. "Now, you feed that fire a bit more, and I'll check it again this arvy."

"Thanks heaps, Beth. See you this afternoon. Whoops, arvy." She gave Min a nudge with her foot to move her out of the way, then followed Beth out to the gate to wave goodbye.

Back in the kitchen, the weight off her shoulders, Grace screwed up her face. "Oh, bugger. I meant to ask Beth who Squire was."

Daniel looked up at her. "I don't know?"

Grace laughed. "Sorry, mate. I was talking to myself. I know you don't know; neither of us does. We'll ask Dad when he comes in. Now, shall we go and unpack all your clothes and toys?"

As they entered the bedroom, a puff of wind and the faintest scent of lavender wafted over Grace. She rubbed the goosebumps on her arms as she turned back towards the door and her ears tuned in to an unfamiliar sound.

If I didn't know better, I would think a long skirt is swishing along the floor?

Reprimanding herself for her vivid imagination, she

shook her head and concentrated on Daniel and the pile of clothes he was hauling out of boxes.

Too tired to bother unpacking the previous night, she had made up the bed in the first room off the massive dining and lounge for them. It held a queen-sized bed, seemingly brand new. Now Beth had filled in the gaps, the new beds had been delivered a fortnight ago. The old double bed and wonky singles with their saggy mattresses had been relegated to the shearers' quarters and the unused foreman's house hiding in the trees behind the woolshed.

She hoped that was a good sign, and that the new owner was serious about bringing the property into the modern era and making it fully functional.

Daniel had slept all night in the small room off the kitchen but was excited about having his own room organised close to that of his parents.

They busied themselves unpacking clothes and toys and dressing the new single bed with jungle-themed linen, before Grace's thoughts once again drifted to Pete.

She crossed her fingers on both hands. *I hope the farm tour is going well. With the amount of time they spent together yesterday, I thought they would have seen it all. If the two of them can work together without Pete letting his fiery temper reveal itself—at least not too soon anyway—we should be okay.*

Absentmindedly, she gently rubbed her sore shoulder again, doubting not for the first time that it had really been an accident. Loading the truck and float with the final few boxes in the darkness, Pete had crashed a heavy box he was carrying into her as they'd met in the doorway. Perhaps he hadn't seen her? Perhaps, like her, he had still been half asleep? Or had it been something more sinister—like a reminder about her being his subservient?

No. She reassured herself that it hadn't been intentional, desperately trying to dismiss the little voices of doubt whispering in her head.

Happy with the organised bedroom, Grace left Daniel to play and wandered outside, seeking a mobile signal in the different areas of the house and garden so she could ring Georgie. Focused on her search, she'd failed to hear Pete arrive sooner than expected, his shadow startling her as he'd stepped out from around the side of the house.

"Who are you talking to?"

"No one yet. I am trying to find a signal so I can use my phone to ring our friends and family."

"Who do you need to call?"

"Just someone to talk to. Let them know how we're settling in."

"Who?" he responded angrily. "And where's my lunch?"

"Oh, sorry. I didn't realise the time. I'll get it ready now. I just wanted to have a chat with Georgie."

He snatched her phone from her hand as his temper flared and threw it across the yard, smashing the screen. In shock and fury, Grace ran at him, flailing his chest with punches as she swore at him. Her blows were like water off a duck's back. Laughing in her face, his eyes flashed with sadistic amusement as he mocked her. Grabbing her shoulders, his brute strength tightened as he held her far enough away to prevent her fists from making further contact.

Fear rapidly replaced her anger, and it was Daniel's call that distracted them both. Pete's grip relaxed, allowing Grace to step backwards and run to her little boy, praying he hadn't witnessed the incident. Pete stormed inside while Grace picked up the shattered phone, pulling a tissue from her pocket and wrapping the phone in it, hoping she would be able to rescue the SIM card.

Gutted by the incident, she would hide it from Pete until her next trip to town. She crossed her fingers and prayed they would be able to repair it but if he found it again, there was no knowing what he would do with it. The phone was her lifeline to her family and friends, and her emotions seesawed between fury and despair.

She smiled at Daniel as she entered the veranda and picked him up, holding him tightly to her.

"Dad's ready for lunch now. Come and help me?"

CHAPTER 5

*G*race blanched, as Pete wolfed down the leftovers of last night's delicious casserole. After spreading fresh bread thickly with butter, he shovelled it into his mouth as though starving. Revolted by his lack of table manners, Grace stood and filled the kettle as she recounted Beth's visit. Her shoulders relaxed – the phone incident was already forgotten. Pete's ability to flip moods so rapidly still flummoxed her.

Sitting and facing Pete, she asked the all-important question. "So what do you think of Tullagulla so far?"

"Not much. It's so bloody dry and neglected, but it does look a bit better as you go to the western end of the property. The cattle are still alive but they don't look great. No one's introduced new bloodlines for years so they're all inbred and in poor condition due to the drought. Plus there's been a wild dog problem out here for a while too, so they've lost a lot of sheep and a few calves. I hope this new owner's prepared to pour a heap of dough into this place. The layout of the property is okay but it seems that Greg and Squire have just been patching things up for years."

"Who's Squire?"

"I haven't met him yet but Greg said he's the station hand. Bit of a loner apparently. Doesn't say much. Lives in the single men's quarters between the woolshed and shearers' quarters. He's been here for years but Greg can't remember where he came from. Turned up in time to help after floods and just stayed. Greg says he's a pretty good horseman so he leaves him to do most of the stock work. Greg concentrates on the tractor work and anything that requires machinery."

"Hmmm, interesting workmates. Are you planning a get together to discuss the priorities? We could email a list of suggestions to the new owner if you like. He probably needs to have a bit of a head's up before he visits." Grace spoke hesitantly, aware her comments could be met with rebuff or sarcastic rejection.

"Yeah, maybe. I'll get the boys to come in after work tonight and we can have a chat. You can take notes." Pete stood, scraped his chair back, and headed out the kitchen door, now focused on having his 'chat' with the fellas.

Her mouth twisted with wry humour, Grace was pretty certain how that conversation would go. *'Come in for a beer and a chat. I've had a great idea.'*

As the ute drove off again, Grace raided the cold room. It contained a veritable smorgasbord of fresh

meat, boxes of vegetables, and a range of dairy prod-
ucts that a country supermarket would be proud of. In
the middle of the large tray of fresh meat, dominating
its diced and sliced companions and taking pride of
place, was a leg of lamb.

"Perfect." She spoke as if the leg was her friend. "I'll
put you in the wood oven with the vegies and you can
be cooking while we have this meeting tonight."

The relief Grace experienced when Beth had
explained that the cold room held the refrigerated
supplies for all of the staff on Tullagulla had been
immeasurable. Confronted by the trays of meat,
numerous blocks of cheese and butter, tubs of yogurt,
and packs of bacon, panic had coursed through her at
the thought she was expected to concoct recipes to use
these ingredients before they went off. It had taken
Beth more than one attempt to get through to Grace
the fact that every time a vehicle drove onto Tullagulla,
its passengers would be lining up for a hot or cold
drink and expect fresh scones or a piece of cake, at the
very least, before they headed off to the next property
or back to town.

Grace was already enjoying being able to wander
into the cold room to select whatever took her fancy.
Rather like having my own little supermarket.

Stepping out of the shower, she glanced in the mirror,
wiping the steam from its glistening surface with the

corner of her towel. Deep green eyes looked back at her, their bright colour dominating her pale, lightly freckled face. She bent forward, rubbing her tangled strawberry-blonde hair with the towel before flicking it back over her shoulder, mentally ticking off some of the questions that needed to be raised with Tullagulla's owner.

Pulling on clean jeans and a crushed but clean shirt, she combed her hair and turned to her son who was still swishing up and down in the shallow bath water, surrounded by an assortment of toys.

"Come on, mate. Your turn now. Out you hop."

She bent to pull the plug out before she helped Daniel wrap the towel around himself, pleased that she had investigated the waste-water disposal. With so little water available, she had felt guilty about using it. However, the discovery of a thick, purple-coloured hose attached to the waste pipe had eased her conscience. At least it drained into the garden and she could move it around to water the trees and shrubs. She had also found that the washing machine was plumbed to the filtered dam water. Not the best for keeping white fabrics white, but great for all the dirty farm clothes, and a big help with conserving the tank water.

At the sound of voices, Grace returned to the kitchen. Pete had his back to her, pulling off his boots as Greg laughed at something he said. A third man stood waiting on the step, his hat in his hands as he solemnly listened to the banter between Greg and Pete.

She pushed the door open, smiling. "Hi." Reaching out to shake his hand, Grace studied the small, thin man with interest. He had a long grey beard, greying hair tied in a ponytail, and a clear olive complexion, confusing any estimation of age.

Clearing his throat before introducing himself, the man nodded shyly. "Good evening, Mrs Campbell. Joseph Gentry. Here they call me Squire." Grace was taken aback by his cultured English voice, more suited to a lord of the manor in the soft rolling hills of England than a station hand in outback Australia.

"Here, Squire," Pete interrupted. "Have a beer."

"Thank you, but no thanks. I don't drink. A glass of water will do me fine."

Pete's face displayed a mixture of surprise and annoyance as he and Greg scraped the chairs out and cracked open their beer cans. Squire's quiet and careful placement of his chair was accentuated in contrast.

Grace fetched the jug of water from the cold room and poured Squire and herself a large glassful each.

While the men settled in, she pushed a DVD into the old player for Daniel to watch and reached for the pen and paper from the bench. Picking up her water, she sat opposite Pete before nudging his leg under the table.

Pete glared at her as he spoke. "Righto, let's get started. I reckon we need to make a list of suggested improvements for Tullagulla, and then we can go through and prioritise them. When the new owner finally shows up, we can show him what needs doing, but in the meantime, he needs to have an idea how rundown everything is."

Both Greg and Squire nodded in agreement.

Greg spoke first. "Well, for a start, we need new fences. It's so long since some have been replaced it's just a free for all out there. The dogs are killing sheep and lambs and the bulls can't be kept separate from the cows 'cause none of the fences are strong enough. The only one that's okay is that new boundary fence with Orden Downs, and they reckon they did that without any contribution from Tullagulla."

Grace bent over her pad and jotted the information down.

They continued for almost an hour, working through a myriad of issues as Pete and Greg swallowed several cans of beer.

With two foolscap pages filled with notes, dot points, and questions, Grace got up and opened the oven door before poking the meat with a large fork.

The delicious aroma wafted over them all, clearly galvanising Greg into action. "Righto, if we're done here, I'm off back to me dear wife to see what's for dinner."

Squire stood quietly and placed his chair carefully under the table, nodding to Grace. He touched his hand to his brow, the hat line across his forehead still obvious. "Thank you very much for your hospitality."

Unsurprised now by his gentle, cultured voice, Grace smiled. Although he had said very little all evening, he'd listened intently, nodding in agreement when required.

He looks like a bushman but has obviously been educated somewhere much more urban. I wonder what his history really is?

It was nearly eleven p.m. when Grace finally finished the email to Tom Lansdowne and signed off as Pete Campbell. She was relieved that she had found the information Pete had handed her when he'd first got the job. The glossy, professional business card displayed the accountancy practice name across the top and in smaller letters below, his name, phone number, and email address. Apparently the official paperwork welcoming them to Tullagulla was still somewhere in transit with Australia Post.

Sighing, Grace hit send and pushed the chair back. After shutting down the computer, she stretched her back, turned off the lights, and headed along the corridor towards the bedroom.

In the silence of the sleeping house, the gentlest of breezes wafted through the lounge blowing strands of hair softly across her face. She crossed towards Daniel's room, her ears tuning in again to what sounded like a long skirt swishing over the timber floor. This time she felt no fear, just intrigue, as the sound faded away. Her determination to investigate Tullagulla's past became foremost in her mind.

"um, Mum, there's a plane coming." Daniel's voice was shrill across the lawn, penetrating the open windows of the old house.

The hum of the engine approaching reached Grace as she met Daniel on the side veranda. The view down the gentle slope to the airstrip was unimpaired, assisted by the years of drought. Daniel leapt up and down, his face alight with excitement as the little Cessna focused on the southern end of the strip, progressively lowering its body before bouncing along the ground and gradually slowing to a halt.

Mesmerised, Daniel and Grace watched until seconds later, the spell was broken by the farm ute rattling past the house and the two-way radio in the office crackled.

"Tullagulla one to base. You there, Grace?"

After running to the office, Grace picked up the

hand-piece and pushed the button as she spoke. "Base here, Pete. Go ahead."

"I'm just picking Tom up. He radioed in while we were in the shed. Over."

Tom? Her mind went blank. "More info, Pete? Over."

"The boss."

"Oh, righto. Over and out."

Her head spun as she raced back along the corridor and threw open the door to the huge master bedroom. Daniel trotted behind, looking at her questioningly.

Of course. Geez, it's only a few days since I sent the email. I thought he'd email back, not turn up like this?

She frantically whipped the dust covers from the armchairs. It took only seconds to check for moths on the floor and dead blowflies on the bed. Throwing open the curtains and windows, she breathed in the fresh air as it wafted through the room before dashing into the en-suite and glancing in the toilet bowl to ensure any lurking frogs were flushed away. The battle to keep the house clean was constant, made more difficult by the need to ration water.

Scooping Daniel into her arms, she ducked into the bathroom and tipped him over the basin to wash his hands and face before plonking him back on his feet. His startled expression reminded her that he had no idea what was going on.

"Sorry, mate. The plane's bringing Tullagulla's new owner to visit us. We didn't know he was coming, so we'd better tidy up now and go and make some morning tea."

Daniel nodded, smiling again, as she dried his hands and face and turned back to the mirror before quickly brushing her hair and tying it in a ponytail.

Glancing through the gauze on the side veranda, Grace studied the little Cessna at the end of the airstrip. Like a patient old bird it faced south, sitting ready for take-off. The ute reached the top of the slope and was approaching the house, the sun reflecting off the windscreen and concealing its passengers.

Ripping the lid off the cake tin in the kitchen, Grace checked its contents, smiling gratefully as she peered down at the delicious big chunk of fruit cake. Beth's creation.

Her own first attempt at a cake had been disastrous and following its cremation, her roast mutton had been equally inedible. It had still been raw. Determination and a good deal of smoke were winning over the infuriating oven as she learned just how much wood needed to be fed into its greedy mouth to get the thermostat to move. Mastering the skill of keeping it at the right temperature was still a challenge—obviously something that took time and practice—and she whispered a silent thanks to Beth for their new arrangement with baking.

The ute doors slammed. Pete pushed under the honeysuckle first, closely followed by a tall, athletic man, considerably younger than she had expected. Clean-shaven, dressed in a checked country shirt, moleskins, and highly polished riding boots, he wore sunglasses, his eyes hidden from the glaring sunshine.

After removing their boots and hats, the men stepped inside the kitchen. Biting her lip in surprise, Grace wrestled with her emotions as her eyes drank in Tom's tight curly hair, neatly trimmed around his neckline and perfectly framing a long, honest face.

Nice, very nice. Overwhelmed with sudden shyness, she studied her feet.

Collecting her wits before raising her head, her smile quivered as she met his stare while the warmth crept up her neck and onto her face.

"Hi. You must be Grace? I'm Tom." His mouth was a wide, welcoming grin and his handshake warm and instantly comforting.

Grace grinned back, allowing her breath to trickle out slowly. Her eyes were glued to his face. His sunglasses gradually adjusted to being inside and she realised they were transition lenses as they lost their tinted appearance. She wasn't quite sure who she'd expected, but he certainly hadn't resembled the person now standing in front of her. As he rolled up his sleeves to just below the elbow, Grace studied the brown, muscly forearms covered in soft, blond hair.

Wow. You certainly aren't my vision of an accountant.

"Sorry to spring this visit on you unannounced, but I got Pete's email and decided that it was time for me to take some action." He gave a short, comforting laugh before continuing in his confident, mesmerisingly quiet voice—another shock to Grace, so used to Pete's raucousness. She was still getting used to the fact that he wasn't at all as she had imagined, not that she had really given his appearance much thought. She'd just assumed he would be older, fatter, and, well, more of a 'boss'.

"My hobby is flying so I rang Civil Aviation and the local airports and organised my route and permits. I've arranged to keep my plane at the Toowoomba airport so I can fly up and down from Melbourne on the commercial flights and then just pop out here in the little Cessna. It took me a couple of days to get here this time though. Had a few stops on the way up." He smiled again, his face alight with interest. "If it's okay with you guys, I thought I would stay a few days and have a look around, chat about what we need to do here, and then head back to Melbourne to get things underway."

Obviously stunned by the pleasant surprise, Pete was slow to react. "Sure. That sounds great. I'll just call and let the fellas know you're here while Grace shows you the house."

"Come on through, Tom. I'll take you to your room first, so you can put your bag in there, and then we can have a further look around."

Tom dutifully followed Grace along the corridor, his eyes swivelling left and right as he took in the home. No doubt hailing from a smart town house or the like in Melbourne, the shabbiness of the homestead would be a stark contrast for the new boss.

"I'm sorry. The bed isn't made up yet as it's never been slept in, but I can do that for you when you are checking out the property."

"Don't worry. I'm quite capable of making a bed, and I certainly don't expect you to wait on me."

Grace looked up at him, surprised. He was serious.

She continued, "This is your bathroom and your veranda. It goes right around the house but there's a little gate at each end of your section, so it can be locked off for privacy if you like. There's no television here, but we do have the satellite dish, thanks to your father, but only the little television out in the kitchen."

"Wow, it really is like stepping back in time, isn't it?" Tom's shock at what he had inherited was obvious.

"Yes, well, we'll get used to it, but it would be good to be able to fix up a few things so life is more pleasant for everyone, including the stock." Grace stopped suddenly, aware that Pete probably wouldn't be happy she'd voiced that, and she bit her lip in anxiety. Tom's immediate response confirmed his understanding.

"I've had a good look through the list Pete sent, and I noticed the house wasn't mentioned, or any of the accommodation actually? Now I'm here, I think we need to address that as well."

Grace smiled. "Thanks. Let's have a quick look through and then have a chat about things with Pete? The kettle will be about to boil, and I bet you are ready for a coffee or tea. That must have been a pretty tiring journey—all the way from Melbourne to Tullagulla in that little plane."

"Certainly am. Yes, my arms are a bit tired, flapping all that way."

Grace's head jerked around and she stared as he

broke into a wide grin. His hazel eyes shone with intel-
ligence and humour and Grace giggled with relief.

After a quick inspection of each room, they returned to
the kitchen just as the kettle began to whistle.

"Perfect timing. What can I do?" Tom's offer to help
stunned Grace. This man was full of surprises.

The tea and coffee made, Grace sat at the table
when Pete arrived with Greg and Squire. With intro-
ductions over and mugs in hand, Grace desperately
tried to concentrate on Tom's questions about stocking
rates, breeding, and commodity prices. It seemed he
wasn't the ignorant landowner Pete had thought he
would be after all.

Daniel interrupted the conversation, showing Tom
his trucks, and Grace's stomach clenched as she shot a
glance at Pete's face. Sitting opposite her, his steely
gaze met hers. It was a silent reminder flashed across
the table that said, *I am the manager here. Don't interrupt
us and remember your place.* A wave of embarrassed
desperation swept through her. Pushing her chair back,
she prepared to distract Daniel and take him outside.

Tom smiled at Daniel, his obvious genuine love of
children defusing the tension in the room. "They're
awesome, Daniel. I'll have a play with you later. I just
need to have a talk with Mum and the men for a while
so perhaps you could get all the trucks ready and lined
up for us?"

Daniel was delighted, scurrying off to assemble his trucks. Grace's stomach unknotted slightly as Tom included her in the discussion.

"Do you mind living so far out of town?" Tom directed his question at Grace.

Squirming in her chair, Grace wished Tom would switch his attention away. Pete's eyes burned into her skin and she sensed his anger mounting. "No, not at all. I grew up on a farm and I love the land. It's a great life for us all, and I'm more than happy to help where I can and support Pete." She hoped that her subtle inclusion of Pete in her reply had reassured him. At least while Tom was here, her husband would keep his foul temper in check.

It was Pete's turn to squirm, no doubt privately annoyed that Tom was dominating the conversation, asking questions about benchmarking, budgets, and projected cash flows and discussing things that Pete didn't really understand. He hadn't been entirely honest in his application for this job, advising the agent that his agricultural degree had taught him everything he needed to know in order to run an efficient property. He didn't think it would matter that Grace was the one who'd actually studied for and earned the degree.

"It's only fair to begin with that you guys know a bit about me so we can get off to a good start," Tom announced. "My father passed away suddenly two months ago and, as his only child, I've now taken over his portfolio of investments. I admit I am still adjusting to the realisation that I own Tullagulla. My father never mentioned the property, and as far as I've been able to make out, I don't think he ever even came here? He wasn't keen for me to help him with his investments either. His motto was 'age trumps education'." Pausing, Tom shrugged as he rubbed the back of his neck before continuing.

"I've had to find out most of my information from the solicitors, so I apologise for the gaps. Hopefully between us all here we can piece it together, make the necessary changes, and get this property back on its feet again. Fortunately, I have an aunt and uncle who own a sheep and cattle property in country Victoria, and I spent a good bit of time as a kid and a teenager staying with them. Not quite the same as here though!"

"Sounds good to me," Pete answered. "Greg's filled me in a bit with Jock's history. He said he was a pretty good manager—it was just a bit tough being able to do what needed to be done without the financial backing this place really needed. Not helped by the last few years of drought either."

"Oh, that's interesting. I haven't been able to find out much about Jock, especially as he and my father passed away around the same time. Tell me more?" Tom leaned forward, elbows on the table, his brow furrowed as he prepared to listen to what Greg had to say.

Greg cast a measured stare around the table and began. "He was here for nearly forty years and was around seventy when he died. Some old fella in town called Henry Dawes knew him pretty well and did the eulogy at his funeral. From what I understand, Jock came from Scotland with his old man as a kid and they did all kinds of farm work together. When Jock's father died, Jock was asked to stay on. Then, Angus passed away and Tullagulla was sold to your father. Jock never left – that is until he was carried out of here in a coffin."

Fascinated, Grace absorbed the information, her thoughts with Jock. She was annoyed when the spell was broken by Pete fidgeting and joggling one knee, vibrating the old floor.

"Why don't you take Tom over to have a look at the machinery shed?" she suggested firmly. "I'll get lunch ready and then we could go for a tour of the property."

"Sounds like a good plan." Tom smiled at her, collecting the empty plates and carrying them to the sink. "I think this kitchen could do with some updating too. What do you reckon?"

"Just a bit." Grace laughed, her stiff, anxious frame relaxing slightly.

"What about me?" Daniel's little voice tremored as the men stood to leave.

"I haven't forgotten you, Daniel." Tom squatted on the floor next to him and straightened one of the lined up trucks. "Do you think we could wait until after lunch? I'm really sorry, but I need to go with your dad now. We'll be back soon though."

Daniel hesitated, his face clouding with uncertainty as his father glowered at him. Turning from one to the other, Daniel remained glued to the spot until Tom reached out and picked him up, once again breaking the tension in the room.

"Don't worry, mate. I won't forget. I promise I will sit and play with you later."

Daniel stared at Tom, his face pale with disappointment, before silently accepting his offer and nodding briefly.

As the gate slammed, Grace turned to Daniel, sitting beside his trucks and loader on the floor, his excitement at having Tom to play with temporarily shattered. Her heart melted as she studied her beautiful little boy. A miniature of his dad in looks, his temperament could not be more different. Crossing her legs, she lowered herself onto the floor and, to Daniel's delight, proceeded to drive a miniature stock truck over a ramp made of books.

As Daniel's imitation of a revving truck penetrated her thoughts, she relived anxiously, the recent incidents involving Pete's temper and their arrival at Tullagulla.

The changes between them now engulfed her. He had been so charming and happy early in their relationship. A chasm was opening between them. She didn't understand why he didn't like her talking to anyone else. Her stomach cramped again.

Grace gazed around the Tullagulla kitchen as Daniel drove a toy truck up her leg and climbed onto her lap. Laughing, she gave him a hug and set him back amongst the toys. Then she jumped to her feet and busied herself preparing lunch for them all.

After quickly chopping onions and vegetables, she beat eggs and poured the quiche ingredients into an old enamel dish and slid it into the hot wood oven before wiping her hands on her jeans. Last night's cold leg of mutton still had enough meat left on it for lunch, so she picked up the sharp butcher's knife and sliced the firm, grey and pink meat before placing each piece in a neat row on the platter.

Nearly as good as a butcher, she congratulated herself.

Rustling through the pantry shelves, she found a jar of what looked like chutney. Opening it, she then tipped the contents into a dish before dipping a teaspoon into the jelly-like substance—first smelling then tasting it cautiously. "Hmmm. Tastes good—even if I have no idea what's in it." She spoke out loud before turning to the bread-maker. After lifting out the loaf tin and turning the bread onto the cooling rack, she inhaled the delicious scent as she covered it with a clean tea towel. While setting the table, she remembered an interesting snippet from the conversation that had taken place in this kitchen less than an hour ago.

Pete had suggested to Tom that they reduce the sheep numbers and replace all the cattle on Tullagulla. The wild dogs were getting worse and Greg and Squire had been going out regularly to set traps and shoot the pests. The feral pigs were also out of control and Grace was sick at the thought of the dogs and pigs getting fat and multiplying at the expense of Tullagulla's sheep and calves.

No one seemed to have any idea how many head of stock were supposed to be on Tullagulla. Neither Greg nor Squire had seen last year's tally book following shearing, and no new stock had been purchased for years. Between the tragic floods several years ago, the feral predators, and the current drought, stock numbers had dwindled and hadn't been discussed with Tom's father.

Probably because no one knew him.

CHAPTER 7

Grace glanced at the clock as men's voices became louder, her excitement mounting at the opportunity for a tour of the property. Just settling in, cooking, and cleaning had dominated her days since arriving at Tullagulla, and she had seen very little outside of the homestead.

After lunch, they loaded into the LandCruiser. With the air-conditioning gently circulating through the vehicle, Daniel was asleep within minutes. Grace pressed against his car seat in the back as Greg leaned forward through the middle of the front seats. Too busy pointing out the different areas of the property and fences that needed priority, he seemed not to notice he was inadvertently pushing Grace aside.

Pete drove, one hand on the wheel while he waved the other around in front of Tom's nose, seemingly unaware of the fallen branches, sticks, and ant hills they bounced over, throwing those in the back seat around like a dingy in a stormy sea. Bumping their way along the rough tracks and stopping frequently, Greg showed them the recently planted but struggling crops, and the lethargic stock grazing on the wiry grasses and the few sparse shoots struggling to emerge through the hard-baked soil. In spite of the rough trip, the drought, and the condition of the stock, Grace was loving every moment.

It is so beautiful—harsh, but beautiful. There were a few inclines and sandy ridges breaking up the mostly flat paddocks, their soil dark and peat-like, morphing to brown, lighter earth as it rose towards the higher ground. Along the dry creek beds stood magnificent old eucalypts and casuarina trees, their green and grey foliage offering much-needed shade. As they circuited the paddocks, kangaroos bounced away. The sheep followed in terror while the cattle heaved themselves to their feet and watched—too lazy, hungry, or tired to be bothered moving. Pete drew to a stop to inspect every windmill, the blades turning gently in the breeze as the bore water pumped up from deep beneath the ground, rhythmically splashing into the trough a few metres away. Without the bore water, Tullagulla would not survive. The old dams were too few in number and were now silted up by repeated droughts and overuse. The shallower ones were empty, dry, and cracked.

Grace studied Tom. His brow furrowed more as his concern seemed to grow and she ached with under-standing. The poor condition of the property was obviously a shock to him. Not only him, but to her as well, in spite of what Pete and the men had already shared.

Tom stayed for a week. Grace's hopes and spirits rose and her confidence grew as plans were made, problems discussed, and some solved. Tom's easy-going nature soothed tensions as they all went about their work.

With him not having to return to Melbourne for a few days, Tom had decided they should do a muster to establish exactly what stock still existed on Tullagulla. Overjoyed with Beth's offer to look after Daniel, Grace prepared to join in. As she prepared food and drink packs in the early dawn, Pete's booming voice dominated the conversation.

"Can you ride a horse, Tom?"

"No, never had the opportunity. My farm experience included motorbikes and tractors, but no horses unfortunately. I wouldn't mind learning though."

Pete either didn't hear or dismissed Tom's comment. "Righto, you get in the ute with Greg and he'll tell you what to do."

Grace cringed at Pete's controlling, derogatory tone. Had he forgotten that Tom was actually the boss, not him? And anyway, Tom was proving to have a lot more knowledge than Pete seemed to give him credit for.

Barely able to contain her excitement, she saddled Jarrah, then Pete's big bay gelding, Ranger, and led them out into the yard where Greg and Tom were waiting in the ute.

Squire was riding along the track towards them on a skittish chestnut, oblivious to its shying at imaginary ghosts behind every piece of scrub. His slight body was at one with the horse, calmly soothing it in quiet tones, one hand on the reins and the other patting its neck, his stock whip draped over his shoulder.

"Greg, you take Tom out to the far paddock we looked at the other day and open the gates as you go. We'll split up when we get there and collect stock around the edges and push them back towards the yards. We'll meet at the gate once the paddock's cleared," Pete ordered.

After grabbing Ranger's reins from Grace, he put his foot in the stirrup and swung into the saddle. For such a big man, he was a relaxed and graceful rider and although tough on his horses, his success in camp-drafting competitions and rodeos was evident in the number of trophies and buckles stacked in the box in their wardrobe.

The three riders trotted side by side for the two hours it took to reach the far boundary, easing only when one of them got a stitch or wanted to have a closer look at something. The ute had gone ahead with the dogs tied to the frame on the tray, their heads reaching to see above the cab as their ears flapped in the breeze.

As the riders arrived at the parked ute, Grace dismounted and unclipped the dogs, calling Min to her.

Tom met her gaze. His face was gentle and encouraging as he quietly spoke. "You look great on a horse."

Grace flushed. "Thanks. I can teach you to ride if you like?"

"Would you? That would be wonderful—thanks."

Grace laughed. "Not just at the moment though. We probably should get on with the job at hand first, don't you think?"

"Probably." Tom laughed. "You're on. As soon as we have time, I'll nag you for a lesson."

Pete's whistle pierced the air and Molly and Tweed flew off the ute tray to his horse's side. As he yelled orders at everyone, Grace tucked her water bottle back into her saddlebag and swung Jarrah to the right-hand side of the paddock. Min galloped next to Jarrah as she broke into a canter.

Not accustomed to regular handling, the stock bolted away from the riders and dogs, gathering in a thick mob as they neared the gate. The older, heavier cows lumbered along, while the healthier youngsters bucked and frisked. In true flock mentality, the sheep clumped together, swirling in a tightly packed group as the dogs circled widely around the outside, keeping them together.

Grace steadied the pace, calling to the stock in a low voice as she kept a respectful distance. Most were weakened by the years of drought, and quickly ran out of energy, happy to ease to a steady walk.

At the crack of a stock whip behind her, she spun around to find Squire having a stand-off with a feisty micky bull. Young males that missed being de-sexed when they were young were dangerous and full of attitude and testosterone. Grace was well aware of the requirement for caution.

Pete joined him, cracking his stock whip in the air several times, alternating with Squire's whip as the bull swung his head from one to the other before deciding it wasn't worth the fight, turned and joined his comrades in the mob.

By the time they had all the sheep and cattle in the paddocks closest to the yards and sheds, Grace was as tired as Jarrah and Min. She and Jarrah hadn't ridden so hard for weeks and had lost a lot of their fitness. Grace patted the mare's neck as she wryly talked to her animals. "I think we had better do a bit more work, hadn't we, girls? Not quite as fit as we used to be."

For two days, they sorted the cattle from the sheep, further drafting and separating the older and poorer stock from the younger and healthier animals. Grace was in her element, and in spite of Sergeant Major Pete throwing orders around, her confidence and happiness grew with the reassurances and compliments from Tom. Sadness washed over her briefly when she reflected that Pete hadn't paid her a compliment of any sort for years. And not for the first time, she second-guessed herself. *How did I get it so wrong?*

CHAPTER 8

*D*esperately needing to replenish the fresh fruit and vegetable supply, Grace planned a quick trip to town while the men were finishing the stock work. It would be a perfect opportunity to pop into the library to see if she could find out more about Tullagulla while Tom was still here.

She booted up the computer and ordered the necessities, hopeful that the order would be in stock, ready to collect by the time she had finished the other errands.

Smiling, a burst of gratitude towards Beth propelled her into action. *That woman is a mine of information, including when it comes to the restocking of the pantry and cold room.*

As the silos on the edge of town became visible, Grace breathed a sigh of relief. It was never easy getting away from Pete. His demands came first and it was only Tom's presence this time that stopped him from either objecting to Grace going anywhere or loading her up with so many errands to run that she would have no time to do anything for herself.

On this visit, her first stop was the Telstra shop to see if her phone could be repaired.

Too early to see the technician, she arranged to leave the phone and call back before she left town.

"C'mon, Daniel. We're going to the library."

Daniel looked at her quizzically, clearly not really sure what that word meant.

They climbed the wide, tiled steps before Grace dragged the heavy glass door towards them. As she steered Daniel around it, they almost tripped over an A-frame chalkboard. Grace stopped to read aloud. "Children's story time. Eleven a.m. and one p.m." She checked her watch. Ten minutes to eleven.

A pleasant red-haired woman watched the two of them enter and removed her glasses, allowing them to dangle from her neck on a black cord necklace. She stepped forward to speak to Grace. "Need help, love?"

"Yes please. I just saw your notice about children's story time?"

"Righto. You're the only child here so far this morning, so you can choose the stories," she gushed to Daniel. "We have volunteers come in to read to the little ones, and today it's Fern's turn. Fern's finished school but hasn't started work yet, so she's helping out here and getting some experience," she gabbled on.

Grace nodded and smiled. She had always thought librarians were quiet, reclusive types. *Obviously not in this case.*

As she led a shy Daniel towards the children's corner, his hand tightened in hers. Fern looked up as they approached. A little surprised herself, Grace knew Daniel hadn't had contact with such a colourful young person. Her hair was striped in rainbow colours, tied in two half-plaits, the bottoms fluffy and thick. She wore a tie-dyed singlet top in strange shades of mustard and her skinny legs were encased in tight multi coloured leggings. It was her face that appeared to hold Daniel's attention the most though. Grace was distracted by the piercings in her ears, nose, eyebrows, and lip. Her pretty blue eyes and clear bright skin were barely noticeable.

"Why has she got fishing hooks on her face?" Daniel whispered, staring at Grace, his eyes huge pools of blue.

"Shhhhh. It's jewellery, not fishing hooks. It's rude to stare," she whispered back, hoping Fern hadn't overheard.

After sitting on the floor, Grace pulled him onto her lap and smiled broadly at the cheerful young face. "Hi, Fern. This is Daniel, and he loves listening to stories."

Fern's decorated face lit up, her demeanour melting Daniel's shyness slowly as he adjusted to his colourful companion. Within minutes, he was transfixed, awe and interest clearly alternating as she read story after story to him, her animation and confidence growing with Daniel's.

Grace stood, whispering to Daniel that she was just going to talk to the lady in charge, and edged silently across to the counter. "I am wondering if you would direct me to the local history section please?"

"Well of course, love. What'ya looking for?"

"The history of a local property—Tullagulla?" She raised her shoulders questioningly.

"Ah, that might depend on what ya want to know? If it's about ownership, you'd be best to get onto the titles office." She looked sceptical. "It's a hard one 'cause no one knows much about Tullagulla. No woman has ever represented it at community events, and as far as most people know, hardly anyone lives there."

"But there must have been women living there at some time, surely?" Grace's optimism plummeted.

"Hmmm. Tell ya what—there's an old fella comes in here every week. Henry Dawes, his name is. Been in the district his whole life, and what he doesn't know about outlying properties isn't worth knowing. 'Specially if you want to know stuff more than twenty years old." She winked and tapped the side of her nose. "Deaf as a post and as old as Methuselah, but he might be able to help you. Word of warning though—he'll be hard to get away from once he gets going." She tipped her head back as she laughed loudly, showing a mouthful of fillings and startling the other library visitors.

"Where would I find him?" Grace was anxious to fit

a visit in today if she could. Her opportunities were few and her trips to town minimal.

"Oh, you can't miss him. Head west as if you are leaving town, then turn left down the last road before the 80 sign. You'll see an old cottage on the right set back from the road with a real nice garden all around it."

"Thanks heaps … Julie." She read the name badge on the woman's ample breast and smiled.

Daniel had settled in for the long haul with Fern and was reluctant to leave. Evidently, the piercings and colours were part of who Fern was, and Daniel was cuddled up to her as if they had been best mates all his life. Grace loved the way children were so non-judge-mental. *If only more adults were the same.*

Dragging a protesting and reluctant Daniel away by the hand, she thanked Fern and they stepped outside into the bright sunlight.

Grace returned to the Telstra shop, her fingers crossed that they'd been able to either fix her phone or give her a temporary loan of one while they sent it away for repair.

Her heart leapt with joy as the spotty-faced young man smiled at her and held her phone out, its broken screen now like new. "It's your lucky day. The techni-cian was able to replace the screen and luckily there was no other damage that a good clean couldn't fix." He handed the phone to Grace.

Tears pricked her eyes with appreciation as she rifled in her bag for her wallet. Having paid for the repair, Grace almost skipped as she left the shop and headed to the supermarket to collect her groceries.

"I'm hungry, Mum." Daniel's plaintive request penetrated her own stomach as they placed the last box of groceries in the car.

"So am I." She smiled and opened his lunchbox for him to eat as they drove.

Snacking on her sandwich, Grace slowed before indicating as they approached the 80 kilometres per hour sign ahead. She swung the steering wheel to the left and onto the gravel road with one hand as she finished her lunch in the other.

They crawled along the gravel road. The old settlers' cottage stood out on the right—tiny, painted white, and surrounded by beautiful neat rows of vegetables and flowers. After pulling up outside, she dusted the crumbs off her jeans and walked around to haul Daniel out of his car seat.

To Grace, the cottage seemed to be smiling. Silent but content in its isolation, there appeared no sign of life. That is, except for a pretty, tortoiseshell cat that rubbed against her leg, purring loudly.

"Hello, pussycat. Aren't you beautiful?" Grace bent to stroke the cat before ambling along the broken pathway, her head swivelling in all directions, in awe of the stunning garden.

"Hello, is anybody home?" Grace called loudly as she knocked on the edge of the fly-screen door, remembering Julie's comment about the owner's deafness.

After knocking and calling out a second time, Grace turned and took Daniel's hand as they stepped onto the path again. "We'll just check around the back in case he's there." They followed the tortoiseshell cat to the side of the house.

In the far corner of the back garden, Grace glimpsed a battered old straw hat, bobbing as if caught on waves in a harbour—up and down, in and out, but going nowhere.

She approached carefully, not wanting to startle him as the bent hat-wearing figure straightened up from amongst the lettuces. He turned towards Grace, rheumy eyes squinting with the effort of trying to recognise his visitor. Shock registered on his face, and Grace apologised, thinking she had given him a fright.

"Hello, Mr Dawes. I'm sorry to visit you without phoning first, but Julie from the library thought you might be able to help me?"

Wiping the worst of the dirt on his trousers, Henry held out a shaky, calloused hand as a gentle smile widened and he introduced himself. "Well, missy. We'd better do this properly. Henry Dawes. You are?"

"Grace Campbell from Tullagulla, and my son is Daniel."

"Well, nice to meet you both. Haven't been out to Tullagulla for many a year. Used to see Jock regularly. He'd have a cuppa with me when he came to town. What brings a pretty young thing like you to see an old fella?"

Her hopes and interest rose as she suddenly

remembered Henry was the person who Greg had said read the eulogy at Jock's funeral.

Grace smiled tentatively, uncertain about being referred to as a 'pretty young thing'. "I was wondering if you knew anything about any women who lived at Tullagulla? Did you know Angus McLeod?"

"Weeell, yes, I did, a little bit anyway. Come inside and have a cuppa with me and we'll have a chat." He looked down at Daniel stroking the cat and added, "Her name's Pansy."

His face had changed. It was alive. Now the initial shock dissipated, he was likely delighted to have someone to talk with. Grace followed him up the steps, pausing at the old concrete tub while she waited for him to wash his hands, and allowing her eyes to adjust to the darkened interior of the cottage. She didn't have the heart to admit she couldn't stay long.

As Grace took a seat facing the old sideboard, she was distracted by a photo in a silver frame. Gasping softly, she stood again before bending to have a closer look at the photo. Two women smiled at her—two generations of peas in a pod. Their likeness was uncanny, and the likeness to herself was a shock. Stunned, she turned to Henry questioningly as he fussed over the kettle in the kitchen.

"Is this your family?"

"Yes, my wife and daughter. They were killed in an accident many years ago."

"Oh, I'm so sorry to hear that." Grace gasped,

embarrassed now at her questioning. Henry appeared not to notice.

"You look a lot like my daughter, Isabelle. She and Jock were to be married but she died only a few weeks before their wedding. Jock never had another woman in his life and always remained my friend. I was pleased about that." Henry was matter-of-fact, his eyes glittering with unshed tears.

What a lovely old gentleman. She guessed him to be in his nineties, possibly even mid to late nineties, his active outdoor life belying his true age.

Henry put the tea pot and mugs on the table and settled into an old carver chair, lined with a threadbare cushion before he spoke.

"Angus McLeod. Hmmm. He was a very angry man. I didn't really know him personally, but Jock always said he was a private, solitary soul who didn't treat his stock very well and apparently treated his staff even worse. He never talked about having a wife himself, but an old indigenous woman who worked at Tullagulla back in the nineteen thirties said he gave her a bag of clothing once. It was full of nice, fine clothes that might have belonged to a lady, and a few other items, those that would have been worn by a small boy."

"So, Angus may have had a wife and child do you think?"

"Ooh yes. There was a photo of a woman and child found in one of the bedrooms when Angus died, so there must have been both at some time. But when, no one knows, and I'm not sure what happened to his belongings."

"Did anyone know their names?"

"Well, someone would've, but they'd be long gone by now."

With the mystery still unsolved, they moved on, their conversation managing to encompass a wide range of subjects. Grace was enthralled and stimulated by the revelation that so much knowledge could be stored in the old man's head. She also appreciated the understanding Henry seemed to have for children's needs as he produced a colouring book and pencils from a drawer in the old sideboard to occupy Daniel while they talked.

Eventually, she stood and helped Daniel from his chair. "Thanks very much for your help. I've really enjoyed our visit."

"Any time you are in town, call in for a chat and a drink. You're very welcome." He paused. "And, of course, I enjoy the company."

Grace resisted reaching out and hugging him, unsure of his reaction.

They said reluctant goodbyes, and she promised to visit again, and left loaded with fresh vegies from Henry's garden.

As she drove down the bitumen, her mind consumed with questions and thoughts, Grace was grateful for the long journey back to Tullagulla. Daniel slept soundly in his car seat and she smiled at his sleeping face, a half-eaten carrot still clutched in his hand.

By the time they pulled into the garage, she was calm and collected, at least outwardly so. She desperately hoped to have a chance to talk to Tom on his own and discuss her meeting with Henry. She doubted Pete would be interested but knew Tom shared her thirst for knowledge of what Tullagulla had been like in days gone by—and who had shared the lovely old homestead.

CHAPTER 9

The night before Tom was to return to Melbourne, they unanimously agreed a BBQ dinner was in order while the evenings remained pleasant but not cold. Winter was not far away now.

Beth and Greg joined the meal, together with Squire. Pete lit a fire on the rustic old plough disk BBQ that sat on a sandstone slab near the cedar tree. Both Grace and Beth prepared salads, and Beth made a delicious pavlova and fruit platter for dessert. While Pete and Greg were supervising the cooking of the meat, turning it regularly and splashing the odd shake of beer on the plate 'for extra flavour', Tom sat quietly next to Grace, a drink in hand.

Uttering a sigh of contentment as the evening shade from the cedar tree encompassed them both, he turned to smile at her. "Not a bad life, is it, Grace?" He winked. "Beats accountancy anyway."

"True. It's nice here at Tullagulla. Sort of gets into your bones."

"Sure does. Tell me, where did that husband of yours learn to ride so well? I gather he grew up on a property somewhere?"

Grace turned to Tom in surprise. "I thought the stock and station agent that interviewed him would have given you all his history and credentials?"

"Nope, nothing—not his fault though. I think the solicitor and I just asked him to employ a suitable person."

"Oh, okay. Well, he doesn't talk about his past much. I'll tell you what I know but he might not like it."

"I'll take full responsibility and keep it just between you and me." Tom smiled and winked again. "Go on."

"He was working as a jackaroo on a large property near Normanton before we met. He grew up in The Gulf Country, with a father who lived his whole life on northern properties, and a mother who was apparently lured by the romantic notion of a position as a governess – being the thing to do back in the late seventies. When Pete was only seven, she must have decided she was sick of struggling with the heat, wet, and isolation of the north, so she just packed up, left a note for Pete and his father, and disappeared on the mail plane.

"Pete spent most of his time with the other station kids. The manager and his wife did their best to include him, but I gather his father increasingly drowned his disappointment in alcohol. He never heard from his mother again and he doesn't even know if she's still alive.

"He went to boarding school in Charters Towers until he turned sixteen, then he returned to the Gulf and to a life of being a jackaroo. Pete's father was a good horseman apparently, and all the station children had horses and did a lot of riding. When Pete's father died, Pete got a job on another station and the other jackaroos laughed at him because he was really fussy with his horses. He took care of their legs and hooves and kept his horses properly fed and shod, while others insisted that their horses were tough enough to go 'barefoot'. It was a different life then, I think, and a pretty hard one. While he was there, he competed at the local rodeo and campdraft and became the main pick-up man at all the rodeos in the north."

"Wow, that explains a bit. No wonder he's a bit prickly—and a good rider." Tom raised his eyebrows.

"Yeh, I guess that's why he's pretty tough … and he expects everyone else to be as well."

Tom looked into Grace's eyes as he spoke. "Being tough doesn't give you the right to take it out on others though. Don't let him wear you down, Grace."

Grace's cheeks burned as she glanced towards Pete anxiously. She didn't think anyone had noticed how Pete treated her and was mortified that she had let him down somehow. "I'm stronger than I look. He's good to me when it's just us." She crossed her fingers and sat on her hands as she lied.

As if sensing Grace's discomfort, Tom changed the subject. "What's a pick-up man?"

"In a saddle bronc or bareback competition there are two mounted riders in the ring as well as the bronc and its rider or cowboy. As soon as the buzzer sounds to indicate the cowboy has made time, the pick-up man rides next to the bucking horse and reaches out to help the rider dismount safely. The hazer is the horse and rider that teams with the pick-up man. He closes his horse against the other side of the bronc, so effectively the bucking horse is sandwiched between the two. And while the hazer releases the flank strap, which is what gives the horse the cue to buck, the pick-up man helps the cowboy get off the bucking horse and onto the ground safely. They all need to be pretty brave and have really good balance – that's people and animals I mean."

"Sounds interesting. We'll have to go to a rodeo so I can see how it all works."

"Yeah. They have a little local competition each year near here so maybe you could combine your next visit with it? I'll find out more about it and let you know." Grace dropped the subject, anxious to tell Tom about her visit to Henry Dawes and disappointed when their attention was broken by Pete's summons before she had even begun. "Grub's up, guys. Meat's cooked."

After jumping to her feet, Grace helped Pete remove the meat from the BBQ and place it in a dish.

She grinned at Tom. "Time to get the plates out. I believe dinner is being served."

Grace woke with a start. It was pitch-dark and she had
no idea how long she had been asleep. Her body stiffened as her breath quickened. Pete was snoring, his
back towards her. There it was again—the soft noise of
a long skirt swishing on the floor and the feeling of
being watched. It was the first time since Tom had
arrived that she had experienced the sensation, but
now she was sure it was not her imagination and felt
no fear. The smell of lavender pervaded her nostrils
and the gentlest touch brushed her arm, as light as a
feather wafting in the breeze. Peace shrouded her,
allowing her to relax, the sense of elevation overwhelming as though she was suspended above her bed.
Then, as quietly and quickly as the awareness had
arrived, it was gone again.

What was that? Who was that?

With all hope of sleep gone, Grace got up, wrapped
herself in her dressing gown and tiptoed to the kitchen.
Clasping a cup of hot chocolate in her hand, she moved
out to the old chair on the veranda and sat sipping her
drink as she watched the sky lighten. The pale pink and
apricot hues on the horizon appeared then gradually
deepened to orange and red as the sun slowly peeped
over the ridge and plains behind the airstrip.

*Red sky at night, shepherd's delight. Red sky in the morn-
ing, shepherd's warning.*

Grace reflected on the old saying. Was there any
truth in it? She rose to return to the kitchen. If it did,

she hoped Tom was able to get back to Melbourne safely. She was sure that flying small planes in bad weather would not be a good experience.

After putting her mug in the sink, Grace tiptoed to the bathroom for a shower, her heart heavy at the thought of Tom's departure.

CHAPTER 10

The sound of a heavy truck changing gear out on the road brought Daniel running to the cedar tree. As it turned into their drive over the newly repaired grid, his shrill voice babbled unintelligibly, his excitement overflowing. Grace met him at the door.

"Mum, it's a truck with a huge 'dozer on the back."

"That's exciting, isn't it?" She smiled knowingly at him. "Better give Dad a call on the two-way, hey?"

After racing into the office, Daniel picked up the hand-piece before handing it to Grace. The men were all out at the western end of Tullagulla, the new fencing materials having arrived the previous week. It seemed that Tom was as good as his word, and improvements to Tullagulla's infrastructure would begin immediately.

"You on air, Pete? Over."

"Yep, gotcha. What's up?"

"Got a truck with a 'dozer on board. Where do you want me to send him? Over."

"Oh, righto. Send him down past the woolshed and tell him to follow the track due west. I'll meet him. Over."

"Will do. Over and out."

Grabbing Daniel by the hand, Grace ran out to the veranda and hauled her boots on before she helped Daniel step into his. As they emerged from under the honeysuckle, the driver greeted them, his huge truck still idling in the middle of the track. She relayed Pete's instructions and the driver climbed back into the cab as Grace turned to Daniel.

"Let's make some pikelets and sandwiches to take to the men. We can go to where the 'dozer is and watch him clean out the dam. What do you think?"

Daniel bounced up and down on the spot. Grabbing Grace's hand, he dragged her back towards the kitchen before she swept him into her arms, giggling.

Within an hour, with Daniel strapped into his car seat and Min on the floor at his feet, Grace drove out to where the men were working. It was a long, steady drive, mostly in low gear due to the roughness of the track. She had overheard Greg asking Pete if he could order parts and was pleased that Tom had given the go-ahead for the rusty old grader to be repaired. At least now Greg would be able to fix all the internal tracks and roads, hope-fully reducing the damage being caused to the farm vehicles. The atmosphere at Tullagulla had dramati-cally improved since Tom's visit, the men relieved to at last have someone take an interest in not only the property, but the staff and their welfare as well.

With lunch over, the men returned to fencing while Grace and Daniel sat under the gum trees. Watching the 'dozer working on the smaller of the two dams in this corner of the property, Grace's heart was full as she studied her son, delighting in his excitement, his eyes glued to the huge machine while the skilled driver worked methodically from the centre of the dam to the outside banks, building and reshaping the walls as the depth was increased. The earthy smell of freshly disturbed ground heightened her senses and she watched, fascinated at the flock of magpies harvesting worms and insects from deep in the broken soil. She leaned her head back and stared up at the shapes and colours of the gum leaves wafting above her. Focusing on a hole in the end of a broken branch, she was intrigued as a pink and grey galah flew into it, setting off a raucous racket of high pitched squawks. She smiled. *Lunch time for the baby galahs too.*

Daniel's eyelids were drooping as Grace gathered up the picnic leftovers, acknowledging it was time to return home. In the distance, kangaroos had gathered under the trees along the edge of the paddock for their afternoon nap, unperturbed by the noise and activity of the men and machinery.

Driving back to the homestead, her hopes rose, contentment creeping through her veins as the joy of living on Tullagulla erased her bruised heart and body.

It was barely two weeks later when the rain arrived. Unexpectedly, and perfectly timed for the newly dug dams, the heavens opened and it rained gently and steadily for almost two days and nights. Precious water trickled into the drains and hollows of the land, flowing more quickly and spreading across the paddocks until it finally reached the dams and creeks. Trees dipped towards the ground, the water soaking into their branches and leaves as the bedraggled stock huddled together on raised areas of the now mud-swirled paddocks.

Initially, the two-way radios and landline phones ran hot between neighbouring properties. Rain gauges had the spiders flushed out of them and children played excitedly in the puddles. Totals varied but as the rain and the bush communication eased, those on the land checked their gumboots for redback spiders, added up the rainfall, and headed out to inspect their animals and properties.

Grace opened Beth's back door. "Cooee, it's only me."

Beth's cheery face peered around the kitchen doorway. "Hi, only me."

"Would you be able to mind Daniel for me please? Pete said they need an extra rider to go around the stock and see what the damage is."

"Oh, love, of course. You'll be needed out there with your horse. No good asking me—I haven't ridden in forty years." She laughed. "Greg's not much better since his riding accident years ago either." Turning to Daniel, she reached out. "Hello, my little friend."

Daniel followed Grace inside, dragging his backpack behind him.

"What happened in Greg's accident?" Grace's curiosity got the better of her.

"Oh, the horse he was riding reared up when a goanna ran across in front of it and they both fell backwards. The horse landed on his leg, smashing it quite badly. He was flown to Brisbane and spent weeks down there in hospital and has never been quite the same since. Well, not him—his leg that is." She broke off laughing as she realised her gaff.

"The girls were only little when it happened but we had nowhere in Brisbane to stay so we just remained behind. That was not long after they put the phones on out here so that was my saviour."

"Oh, how awful." Grace cringed with compassion, her thoughts not just with Greg, but with poor Beth stuck here on her own with the children, her husband hundreds of kilometres away.

Daniel's booming voice interrupted the thoughts and memories of the two women. "I'm all ready and I've got trucks, so we can play."

Both smiled indulgently at the little boy as Grace digested the day's plan and waved goodbye.

CHAPTER 11

*W*ith the rain arriving so unexpectedly, the sheep were still in the lower-lying paddocks. The sandy ridge at the back of the property was the safest place for them in wet weather but knowing feral pests were taking weakened sheep and any calves that arrived, Pete had made the decision to leave them in the paddocks closer to civilisation. Grace was surprised, and pleased, when she overheard Pete asking Greg for his opinion on the best way of managing the movement of the stock now that it was so wet.

"Using a vehicle in these first few days won't work. We'll just get bogged. In a few days we might be able to manage with a motorbike if we had one, but for the moment, the only way we're gunna get around this property will be on horseback," Greg announced.

They rode in pairs, with Pete and Greg heading to the western edge of the property to check on the cattle and see how much water had flowed into the newly dug dams. After hearing about his accident, Grace was concerned for Greg and had quietly saddled Pete's old horse for him. He would be safe on Spike and they could concentrate on the cattle and the sections of the ancient boundary fence that were rusty and weak.

Grace rode quietly alongside Squire as they traced the bore drain from the 150-hectare house paddock to the south where the river that had been dry for the past four years now flowed ferociously, its swirling waters muddied and menacing.

Squire's eyes scanned the horizon like an eagle's until quite suddenly he kicked his horse into a canter and headed towards the murder of crows cawing raucously ahead. Jarrah sprang after him as Grace strained to see what Squire could, and that she couldn't.

As they drew closer, the breeze changed direction and the overpowering stench confirmed her fears. A flock of sheep were bogged, weighed down with full sodden fleeces. Those not already drowned struggled feebly as they tried to extract themselves from the clutches of mud and tangled wire. Squire dismounted and indicated to Grace to do the same as he removed ropes and wire cutters from his saddlebag.

"Watch me and then do the same with your rope." he spoke calmly and quietly as he approached the sheep.

Lying on his stomach, Squire reached into the mud. After attaching a loop of the rope around a sheep, he inched back to dry ground, dragging the animal to safety before cutting the tangled fence from its weakened body. Then he did it all again. Holding each sheep up on its feet long enough for the circulation to return, he then cautiously released the animal, waiting patiently for it to either stagger away slowly or spring in terror. Some were too weak to walk or stand, so were pulled into the shade of the belah trees in the hope they would find strength as their fleeces dried out. Grace was relieved that the rain had stopped, the sun now shining through the clearing clouds.

Following Squire's lead, Grace gasped as the cold water soaked through her shirt and jeans.

Too exhausted for tears as the last sheep was dragged to safety, waves of relief and worry consumed her. The rescued sheep huddled together under the trees. Grace wiped the flies from her face, the mud spreading farther as she tried to clean it off with her shirt tail. Squire was also covered in mud and was minus one boot. Grace smiled ruefully, recognising a mirror image of herself.

Darkness was closing in by the time Squire rescued and pulled his recently located boot from the mix of mud and wire. They mounted silently and turned towards home. Grace's shoulders slumped and her stomach growled with hunger.

"Tomorrow we'll follow the water course along and see what else is trapped, but I think we have seen the worst of it." Squire's gentle cultured voice penetrated her fuzzy mind as his gaze met hers. "Don't take it to heart too much, Mrs Campbell. This is a harsh country, and no one expects heavy rain around here at this time of year. God knows it's been a long time since we saw this amount in one event."

The days progressed, filled with more of the same. While Pete and Greg concentrated on the fences and cattle, Grace and Squire repeated the pattern of their first day, thankful that the losses were not as bad.

After hosing the mud off outside when they returned, Grace staggered inside to enjoy a hot shower and clean clothes. As her aches increased, so did the pile of muddied garments on the concrete floor of the laundry. Her love and gratitude towards Beth doubled as she was greeted each evening with a burning wood stove containing a hot meal.

With Jarrah and Squire's young horse showing signs of exhaustion, Squire brought the station horses into the yards and selected a fresh mount from the mob for himself. He suggested Grace ride Beau, a sway-backed older bay gelding. "He ambles, Mrs Campbell."

"Please, Squire, call me Grace." He made no comment and she wasn't sure if he'd heard her.

Grace vaguely remembered reading a childhood story about a horse that ambled but had never understood what that meant—until Beau. After the initial surprise and feel of the pace, something between a fast walk and a smooth running gait, Grace relaxed, unable to wipe the smile from her face. Her enjoyment in riding Beau almost, but not quite, erased the horror of the past few days.

As they rode side by side, Grace's respect for the quiet gentleman grew.

"Squire, would you mind if I called you Joe, and please, call me Grace, not Mrs Campbell?"

Squire's gaze rested on her for a minute before he replied, "Mrs Campbell, Grace." He smiled, his face softening. "Apart from Beth, we haven't seen any women on Tullagulla much. I guess I have forgotten how to talk to the gentler sex. But I think it will be best if we stick to Squire. I have grown used to it after all these years and I really don't mind. If you start calling me Joe, I might just ignore you and then we'll both be in trouble."

"Well, I hope that's not true, Squire. I would be happier if we were a little less formal but I understand what you are saying. We have to work together, after all, and I'm grateful for your years of experience and guidance. I wonder how Beth has managed?"

They studied each other silently for a few seconds before Squire answered. "I think that telephone runs red hot to her family. It's her lifeline to her children and Greg is a good man. It also helps that she knows no other life."

Grace nodded. As an introvert herself, she understood Squire's need for peace and privacy, and yet found him increasingly intriguing. She smiled, pondering for the umpteenth time what his history was. Maybe one day he would tell her?

As the horses strode out, her mind returned to the job at hand and the awful stock losses.

Tom would return as soon as he could safely land his little plane, and she wanted to be able to give him a much more accurate picture of Tullagulla's position. The notebook in her top pocket was full of numbers and notes—the tally of dead stock from each mob and the estimated number of survivors. She didn't know how she felt. On one hand, she was looking forward to seeing him again, and on the other, dreading her role as bearer of such bad news.

CHAPTER 12

*I*t was pitch black when Grace slipped out of bed, staggering sleepily across the huge living room towards the bathroom. As a whisper of breeze wafted past her, there was the noise again—the swishing of a long skirt. The night was cold and she rubbed the goose bumps on her arms. Unsure whether it was the cold or the strange presence that caused them, she puzzled over it again. *Who is there?*

After peeping into Daniel's room, she tiptoed to his bed and pulled the tangled blankets over his shoulders, tucking the edges firmly under the mattress. Reassured there was no one in the room now except the two of them, she ducked into the bathroom before closing the door silently behind her. She drew a slow, deep breath and turned on the light. Had someone been there? Was there a Tullagulla ghost? Should she wake Pete? Uneasy now, she climbed into bed and lay awake, tossing and turning, eventually dozing as the pale dawn crept into the room.

The floor squeaked as Pete thumped out of bed. Her eyes bleary, the opportunity to share her thoughts was foremost on her mind. Hesitantly, she relayed the events of the previous night.

"Are you a raving idiot? There's no such thing as a ghost. You'd better go and see the doctor next time you go to town. He'll agree with me. You've got mental problems."

Furious at herself for mentioning it, she cooked and ate breakfast in silence. Daniel was still asleep as Pete strode to the gate, thrust the honeysuckle aside and ducked under its invasive fronds before disappearing out of sight. Grace bit her lip and took slow breaths, desperate to quieten her thumping heart. Pete's interpretation of her mental state was much more disconcerting to her than his dismissive behaviour over the ghost.

Later that morning she was mopping the floor, her back to the veranda, when Pete burst into the kitchen.

"Don't walk on the wet bits," Grace pleaded. "You're putting dirty marks all over the section I've just washed."

"Shut up and stop your whinging. Tom will be here any minute and I need to ring Bill over at Camden Downs about the campdraft. He called me on the two-way and asked me to give a hand."

Grace gritted her teeth, determined not to get angry before Tom arrived. She quickly re-mopped the marks on the floor and threw an old towel down before shoving it around with her socked feet in an attempt to dry it quickly.

Darting backwards and forwards, Grace set the table for lunch, stirring the thick pea and ham soup on the wood stove as she passed. Her ears pricked up as she tuned in to Pete's side of the telephone conversation.

It was Thursday and the campdraft and rodeo were to start on Saturday. Due to the recent harsh conditions, entry numbers were down as the committee struggled to find enough suitable cattle.

"Yeah, Bill, I'm happy to give a hand. Whad'ya want help with?"

He paused, obviously listening.

"Well, yeah. I can help pen 'em up. Y'know I am having a run myself though?"

Silence again.

"Righto, I can do that. See ya tomorrow then."

The phone slammed back into its cradle before the chair scraped along the floorboards and Pete's broad frame appeared in the doorway. "Looks like Greg dobbed me in to be pick-up man at the rodeo."

"Oh, happy about that?" Grace raised an eyebrow. Of course he was.

"Yeah, why not. I'm in the draw early for my run and Ranger loves the pick-up work. I'll have to go there in the morning though. Help draft the cattle and get organised. The guys are going to set the temporary yards for the rodeo in case the campdraft runs over time. Should be okay. They only have sixty entries and the cattle have been getting hand-fed so they're pretty quiet."

"I thought it was better that the cattle are not too quiet?" Grace was puzzled. "You always say they run better if they're a bit feisty?"

Shrugging, Pete responded, "We'll just have to see, won't we?"

The sound of an approaching plane interrupted their conversation and Pete grabbed his hat as he strode outside.

Butterflies danced in Grace's stomach as the ute returned. Such a lot had happened since Tom was last there. He had phoned almost daily, Pete keeping him informed about the rain, flooding, and loss of stock, but it wasn't the same as experiencing it for himself.

After discussing Tom's riding lessons with Squire, Grace chose to use Jarrah. She was the quietest of all the horses and although not very big, she was strong, and Tom would gain more confidence on a slightly smaller horse.

"Hello, little lady." Tom's wide mouth beamed from ear-to-ear as he gave Grace a gentle hug.

Grace squeezed Tom briefly in return, the heat creeping up her neck and onto her cheeks. She turned to pick Daniel up as he raced into the kitchen.

"Hi, Tom. Can I have a ride in your plane?" Daniel's high-pitched voice side-tracked Tom and he reached out to take the little boy from Grace, allowing her to step over to the stove, her flushed face cooling slightly in spite of the steam rising from the hot soup.

"You're not going in Tom's plane." Pete's noisy entrance rapidly dispelled the joy in the kitchen as he snarled at Daniel. Turning away from his son's stricken face and quivering lip, he continued, "Right, let's eat so I can get Tom out to see the damage before the day's over."

"Let Tom put his bag away first and get changed," Grace retorted, glaring at Pete, annoyed at his lack of social skills and empathy for his own son.

Tom appeared surprised, possibly embarrassed for Grace.

Recovering quickly from his outburst, Pete was still on a high about being asked to help at the campdraft, and for once Grace was glad he dominated the conversation as they ate. Internally she still boiled over Pete's behaviour. However, outwardly she was composed, listening intently and disappointed now that she had decided not to enter the ladies draft. It was so soon after the rain and all the subsequent work that she'd thought Jarrah needed the rest.

Oh well. At least I'll be able to spend the day with Tom while Pete's busy—and answer his questions with a bit more patience and understanding than Pete would. Her heart leapt with hope.

The sun was barely peeping over the horizon when Pete changed gears in the truck as he drove past the homestead, clearly focused on nothing else but the campdraft.

His absence and the promise of a fresh, glorious winter's day boosted Grace's spirits. Today was all hers —a chance to teach Tom to ride, to spend time with Daniel, and to weed the vegetable garden that she had been nurturing for the past few weeks. Her freckles had faded under the healthy glow on her usually pale face. Revelling in the cooler weather, a sense of peaceful joy washed over her. Giving a little skip, she turned to the house before leaping up the steps onto the veranda.

Daniel had taken Tom to visit the chooks, their recent acquisition following major repairs to the ancient shed and yard.

Grace could picture Daniel picking up his pet Pekin chicken and handing her to Tom for a cuddle. He had named her Lisa. Grace had suggested Henny-Penny, but no, Daniel had been insistent that she was called Lisa.

"We're back." The veranda door flew open and Daniel's excited voice signalled their return as she put away the last of the breakfast dishes.

"Sorry about the damage. A slight incident here." Tom winked as Daniel handed Grace the bucket of eggs, now covered with the yellow yolk of the broken one on top.

"A bit too much swinging of the bucket again hey,

Daniel?"

"Sorry, Mum—was an accident." Daniel looked up at her, an anxious shred of guilt on his little face.

"No worries, mate." Glancing at Tom, she added, "It happens quite regularly," and laughed as she bent and gave Daniel a squeeze.

"Did you introduce Tom to Lisa?"

Daniel nodded enthusiastically as Tom gave her a smile and winked. Grace changed the subject.

"Right, let's get our boots and hats on. We are going to teach Tom how to ride today."

Daniel's high-pitched voice chatted all the way to the stables, his excitement contagious. Tom lifted him onto his shoulders as Grace greeted Jarrah and Spike.

After leading Jarrah out into the round yard, Grace sat Daniel on the gate post while she instructed Tom to mount and how to hold the reins.

"Feel comfortable?" she asked.

"I think so. As comfortable as a man can feel when sitting astride an animal as tall as a giraffe anyway. Not to mention the potential time bomb waiting to go off underneath me," Tom joked.

A worried frown formed on her forehead as Grace studied his face. *He must think Jarrah is unpredictable?*

"Don't worry, Jarrah is really kind and trustworthy. She won't do anything wrong." She reassured him.

"I'm just kidding, I feel fine." He hastily comforted Grace with a smile that had her stomach turning backflips. She chided herself and focused on the lesson. *Get a grip on yourself girl, you're a married woman and shouldn't be thinking this way.*

"Okay, I am just going to let this lunge rope out and Jarrah will walk around the outside of the arena until you get the feel and rhythm of her."

Within minutes, Tom had relaxed, Jarrah's patient temperament giving him enough confidence to try trotting. With long legs cuddling Jarrah's belly, Tom barely bounced as her smooth trot carried him in large circles.

"Now try lifting your bum out of the saddle every couple of strides. You'll feel the rhythm as you stand in your stirrups and it will be more comfortable for both you and Jarrah," Grace called.

After a few more laps of bumping gently in the saddle, they were both delighted when Tom suddenly grasped the rhythmic action of rising to the trot.

"I'm going to take the lunge rein off now. Jarrah won't do anything you don't want her to do so just squeeze your legs on her sides and talk to her. When you want to trot, just tell her to trot and see how you go."

An hour later, Tom slithered to the ground and patted the little mare, his grin as wide as his face. "That was awesome. Thanks heaps. I think I might have found some muscles I didn't realise I had but I really enjoyed it."

"You're actually a pretty natural rider. We'll have you out mustering with us in no time." Grace grinned at him as she buckled Daniel's helmet under his chin and threw him in the saddle for the short ride back to the stables. "You've been a very patient boy, Daniel. Now you can show Tom how you ride."

Daniel picked up the reins and smiled at them as his little legs flapped against the saddle. Jarrah lowered her head and walked on slowly and evenly as she completed one last lap of the yard and headed for the stables.

"Jarrah's so good. She just knows he's a little child and takes such care of him. If she feels him slipping to one side, she stops and waits for him to scramble back on properly. I'd love to get him a little pony of his own, but I haven't really had a chance to look around for one. He usually just sits in front of me when we go for a ride."

"Well this is the perfect place for him to have his own pony. He must get a bit lonely for kids of his own age?" Tom questioned.

"Yeah, he does, and I feel quite guilty at times. Next year he'll be able to go to the kindergarten that's held each week at the local hall. It's a fifty-kilometre drive to get there, but it's only one day a week and he'll love it. By then I'm hoping we'll be in a better routine here too and will know more of the neighbours so I might be able to share the driving with one of the other mums."

Tom smiled at her as he helped unsaddle and brush Jarrah down. "Does Greg ride?" Tom asked.

"He tries not to, but he did after the rain came. It was either that or stay at home because the ground was too boggy for a vehicle. If there had been a motorbike here he possibly would have been able to ride that."

"Hmm. Looks like I need to look at that issue then." Tom mused, before Grace continued.

"Anyway, he managed by riding old Spike. Beth told me he had a bad accident some years ago and broke his leg badly. That's why he walks with a limp now. He's really interested in the machinery though and seems to have done a pretty good job on the cropping and hay side of things here."

"Yes, he's taking me out this afternoon to have a look at the crops. Considering they were only planted after that little shower in April, it's amazing they've held on. Hopefully now we've had this latest downpour, we might actually get a decent yield. That is, if it hasn't been washed away or drowned. I know it'll be dependent on getting some follow-up rain too, so it's all a bit of a gamble, isn't it?"

"Farming generally seems to be a gamble. Such a good lifestyle though. I can't imagine any other life," Grace responded thoughtfully.

Tom raised his eyebrows and nodded before bending over and swooping Daniel into the air, settling the giggling bundle of energy on his shoulders as they made their way back to the house.

The winter sun soaked through Grace's clothes as she bent, weeding the garden while Daniel played in the dirt under the cedar tree. Tom and Greg had gone in the farm ute and she hadn't heard from Pete. She doubted he would even think about them. He would be in his element, surrounded by like-minded men. With the truck to sleep in and his swag on board, he would stay on the grounds tonight before competing tomorrow, and she, Tom, and Daniel would head over to the grounds after breakfast to cheer him on and watch the day's events.

She'd barely caught sight of Squire since their stock recovery expeditions following the rain. Wryly, she guessed Pete had allocated him jobs that he wasn't prepared to do himself. The next major event on Tullagulla's calendar would be shearing. Pete probably hadn't thought to ask Squire to get the shearing shed and quarters ready.

On the other hand, why would Pete think about what's best for Tullagulla? Leave all that stuff to the underlings while you have a great weekend doing what you enjoy most.

Grace sat back on her haunches, guilt flooding through her, ashamed of her thoughts. She swallowed, took a deep breath and questioned herself once more.

I don't really mean that, do I? I don't think I like the person I am becoming.

CHAPTER 13

*L*eaning on the rails of the arena, Grace glanced around the crowd. A sea of blue jeans and Akubra hats were facing the ring, brightly coloured shirts and warm oilskin vests breaking the pattern as riders warmed up their horses and a pall of dust rose from the ground. Two men, nonchalantly mounted on well-built stock horses, their whips draped over their shoulders, walked past the crowd on the inside of the rails, chatting quietly to each other. Grace jumped as Tom spoke.

"What do those guys have to do?"

"Oh, they're the stockmen who round up the cattle after each competitor's run and guide them to the yards on the other side of the ring. It's important that the competitor in the ring only has his or her chosen beast to have to worry about."

"Beast. It's a strange term really, isn't it?" Tom commented thoughtfully.

"Yeh, I guess so. Cattle beast. It's generic and just easier I suppose."

Pete was seventeenth in the draw. The cattle were bellowing in the yard, stamping and pawing with confusion as they waited with no knowledge of what they were waiting for.

Tom's gaze turned to the ring as the loudspeaker crackled and the commentator introduced the first competitor. Grace strained unsuccessfully to see the rider working the beast in the cut-out yard, but within seconds the gate was flung open and a healthy young steer galloped into the arena, hotly pursued by the horse-and-rider combination.

The rider's eyes remained glued to the cattle beast's movements. His horse wove behind and alongside it as the rider guided them around the cloverleaf course at a flat gallop. After turning around the second peg, they headed straight for the final obstacle of the course—an open space as wide as a vehicle gate, marked on either side by a post topped with a flag or, in this case, small eucalypt branches instead of flags. The rider desperately tried to guide the steer through the final gate. A disappointed gasp went up in the crowd when, at the last moment, the animal swerved and dived sideways just before the obstacle, missing the gate altogether. The judge cracked his whip, indicating the disqualification of the rider, before the loudspeaker crackled again as the announcer read out the score: forty-two.

"It's not as easy as it looks, is it?" Tom turned to Grace.

She shook her head and chuckled. "It certainly isn't."

"How do they score it?" he asked.

"Twenty-six points are allocated to the rider for the choice and management of the animal he selects from the 'camp' or mob of cattle in the cut-out yard. Then the course itself is worth four points and the success and skill of the rider to get the beast around the full course and through the final gate is worth another seventy points. So, a hundred points all together. In this case, the rider must have done a pretty good job of selecting and working the beast in the camp, but then because he only got around the second peg and not through the final gate, he lost points for not completing it."

"Oh, that's quite tough then."

"Sure is. It's great to watch some of the really experienced stockmen though. They make it look so easy and command a lot of respect."

Tom, Grace and Daniel remained at the rails as rider after rider failed to complete the course. By the time Pete's name was announced, there had only been three successful competitors, and Grace's stomach flipped with nervous excitement. Four of the riders hadn't even made it out into the arena, the selected beast having turned back into the mob, triggering elimination.

A cloud of dust hung over the yard as Pete worked his chosen beast, separating it from the mob of cattle and weaving back and forth until it turned its tail to him, ready to run. The gates were flung open and Ranger jumped into a gallop, tailing the steer, his neck stretched out, oblivious to anything except the animal in front of him. Bent over the front of the saddle, Pete's focus was at one with that of his horse. With him barely moving in the saddle, they rode alongside the steer, swinging it to the left around the first peg before guiding it in a full gallop across the ring to the second peg. As they rounded the marker, Ranger overtook the steer, guiding it towards the final gate, easing back and pushing forwards, weaving alternately until it galloped at full pelt between the final two pegs. A cheer went up from the crowd as the loudspeaker announced, "Good round from Pete Campbell and Ranger. We'll just wait for the score." There was a pause for a few seconds, before he continued, "Eighty-eight. That's a good score for Pete and puts him in the lead."

Daniel clapped in delight, joining in as the crowd whistled, and cheered. "Did Daddy win, Mum?"

"Not yet, sweetie-pie. He did really well, but there are still a lot of riders to go so we just have to wait and see."

By the time they had wandered around the various stalls, had a drink and a hamburger, and visited the bathrooms, the final five riders were lined up waiting to ride and the results would be announced shortly. They had briefly caught a glance of Pete as he helped pen up more cattle and had walked passed Ranger patiently snoozing while tied to the side of their truck.

Grace held Daniel's hand as she pointed towards

the grandstand. "Shall we go and have a seat up there for a while, Tom?"

"Sounds good to me. My legs are just about to cave in after their workout yesterday. Not to mention my rear end." He laughed, strolling gingerly beside Grace.

"Well, this looks like a cosy little threesome." Pete's sarcastic explosion shattered the atmosphere and Grace's happiness plummeted into her boots.

"Daddy." As they spun around to face Pete, Daniel ran to him, laughing and reaching to be picked up.

Pete swung him roughly onto his hip, his eyes fixed on Grace's face.

Tom cast a sideways glance at Grace, anger flashing momentarily across his own. "No need to speak like that, mate. Your wife and son have been introducing me to your world, and I have to say, I'm pretty impressed. That was a great ride." He smiled, defusing the sarcasm and subtly changing the subject.

Pete grinned, visibly content as the rebuff went straight over his head. "Yeah, it was a pretty good run considering the cattle. They're not the best for the job but we can't help that. Have to be able to just read them and make the most of it."

Tom nodded. "We were going to get a seat on the grandstand so we can watch the presentation. Looks like you'll most likely be in the line-up for a placing, so we're your cheer squad."

"Yeah, hope so. I think the last rider's out there now. I'd better get back to my horse just in case." He let

Daniel slide to the ground, straightened his hat, turned and walked away.

Grace took Daniel by the hand and smiled at Tom. "Come on, let's grab a seat."

Pete ended up in third place overall and, happy with his results, Grace breathed a sigh of relief.

With the campdraft over, the men were busily setting up the arena for the rodeo. Delicious aromas wafted from the campfire cooking area, reminding competitors and spectators alike of the evening meal coming up later.

The truck had unloaded the broncs into the yards where an hour ago, cattle had been bellowing. As they walked back down towards the yards, a truck packed with bulls for the main event, the bull ride, drove past the spectators.

"It's the bulls, Mum." Daniel hopped up and down excitedly. "Can we go and see them?"

"Sure, lets. Do you mind, Tom?" she asked.

"Absolutely not. This is all new to me and I'm loving it. Good having a personal guide too." He winked as his grin spread over his face.

Grace melted. He was so genuine and kind. Pretty easy on the eye too. He was not like Pete's dark and rugged type of good-looking. Pete was moody and, well, messy—a bit like an unmade bed. Tom was just attractive. He had such a nice face—a happy, contented face with a smile that seemed to come from nowhere. Tall and slim, his shirts even stayed tucked into his jeans and his Akubra hat wore just enough stains to look interesting.

She was still a bit mystified that he was Tullagulla's owner. For some reason she had pictured an overweight, middle-aged man who would be officious and demanding. She had been really, really wrong, and her mouth twisted as her body flushed warm with unexpected thoughts.

The rodeo started late in the afternoon. The ladies barrel race was up first, followed by the buckjump events, and lastly, the bull ride.

As they pushed through the crowd to where the campfire meals were being served, Grace turned to Tom. "Well, what did you think?"

"Great. It was great," he repeated. "I'm glad you explained it to me though. Actually, the bit that impressed me most was how Pete and that other fellow made the picking up of the cowboys look so easy. Also, those bulls. It's incredible how docile they were in the yards with their owner strolling around them, scratching and brushing them, then they come out into the arena bucking and twisting like gymnasts."

"Yeah, same as the broncs. They are mostly really docile and love performing. As you noticed, they'll only buck when the flank strap or rope's put on. It's like it's their cue for doing what they have to in their job. Some broncs actually get tired of bucking eventually. I had a friend at pony club who had an ex-bucking bronc. He just got tired of bucking but he was so athletic he made a super show jumper."

Tom sat Daniel on his shoulders as they stood in line, waiting to collect their dinner. "It's crowded now, isn't it? Getting noisier too."

"Yeah, the bar's been open for hours and everyone's relaxing and socialising. I doubt many will go home tonight. Most will camp in their trucks or floats, and there will be a few sore heads in the morning when they're trying to pull down the arena." Grace laughed.

"I'm happy to drive home if you would like to have a drink." Tom offered generously.

"No, it's okay, thanks. You have a drink if you want to? I'm happy with a lemonade. Since having Daniel, I don't drink much anymore—unless I'm having dinner with friends or something like that."

"Okay then. I'll just get myself a beer and you both a lemonade?"

"Thanks heaps." Grace smiled as she reached out and took the plate of food being handed to her.

As they pulled into the vehicle shed late that night, Tom reached for Grace's hand before giving it a friendly squeeze.

"I've had a great few days, thanks to you. I'm not looking forward to heading back to Melbourne on Monday, but I'll return in a couple of weeks for shearing."

At Tom's touch, electricity bolted through Grace, sending her heart into a gallop. "I'm glad you enjoyed your weekend. Thanks for keeping Daniel and me company. I really enjoyed it too," she whispered, squeezing his hand in return, willing the peaceful, caring feeling to go on forever.

Grace tossed and turned that night, unable to sleep. She couldn't stop comparing her husband with Tom and accepted she had been in denial about her marriage. Now she had met Tom, she was reminded so clearly of how it felt to be with a man who treated her kindly. He didn't hurt her. He didn't even yell at her or try to manipulate her. In the safety of darkness, she asked herself the question that had been running interminably around in her head.

So why am I still here?

As Tom's plane climbed into the sapphire blue sky in the early Monday morning light, Grace stood under the cedar tree waving with both arms. With the emptiness inside her spreading to her limbs, her energy drained swiftly and her arms dropped to her sides. Tom dipped the wings slightly before flying over the house and away to the south and she let herself collapse on the grass. She remained frozen until the Cessna was a mere speck in the sky, waiting for the blood to flow so her legs would carry her back inside.

CHAPTER 14

*T*he shearers were due to arrive as the wind changed and cold southerlies blew across the now green paddocks. Pete had been in a bad mood for days and Grace was doing the egg-shell walk again. It didn't matter what she or Daniel tried, it was wrong and caused friction. She had left Daniel with Beth the previous day while she'd cleaned the shearers' quarters. *That should please Pete.* She hoped so anyway.

After stomping up the path to the kitchen, Pete threw his hat on the table and met her eyes. Grace's stomach flipped and tripped.

"I told Squire to clean the shearers' quarters," Pete ranted, his face so close to hers she could taste his anger. "Why are you constantly undermining my authority? Squire is a lazy bastard and he does not need my *darling wife* helping him to do HIS jobs."

"Pete, stop it. It's not physically possible for anyone to get both the woolshed and shearers' quarters ready and cleaned in the timeframe we had—as well as bringing the sheep closer and getting them drafted. I know that, and you should too. We need to all work as a team. Why can't you just be grateful that I'm trying to help you?"

"Hi, Dad." Daniel drove his wooden stock truck into the kitchen from the corridor, the cheery smile on his face rapidly draining away as he looked from one parent to the other.

"Hi, mate." Pete turned from Grace and she released a slow and silent breath.

"Do you want to play with me?" Daniel asked hopefully.

"No, son. I was just checking with your mum that everything's ready for the shearers. I have to get back down to the shed now."

To Grace's relief, his mood had improved by dinnertime and he was his old self with Daniel, watching him build with his Lego and actually piggy-backing him to the bathroom and to bed. She'd leave her offer to help with the yarding until the morning.

As she entered their bedroom, warm and smelling of fruity shampoo and toothpaste, Pete wrapped his arms around her. "I know I've been a bit bad-tempered lately. Hopefully when Tom gets here we'll hear what the latest plans are with these sheep. It was a busy time with the campdraft last time he came."

Grace studied his face, drawn into his mesmeris-ingly blue eyes. "I want to help. Please don't ignore me.

You know I could do more with the sheep. I feel as though my qualifications are just being wasted."

He stared down at her, his expression changing to anger as his mouth clamped tightly shut and his eyes flashed. Grabbing her arm tightly, he shoved her against the bedroom wall. "Just remember who you are and why you are here with me."

Grace was totally confused.

His anger dissipated as quickly as it had begun. He picked her up and lay her on the bed before kissing her as he opened her dressing gown and pulled her pyjama top over her head.

Drifting into submission, misery dulled her senses. It seemed that it didn't matter what she did or didn't do. She couldn't win.

As she and Daniel collected eggs from the henhouse, Grace's mind recounted the previous evening and their urgent lovemaking. She tenderly touched her arm where the bruise was turning from pale to dark purple and was glad it was winter. Her thick jumper and shirt covered her arms and her warm dressing gown had given her a small amount of protection against Pete's strong, vice-like grip. It seemed he was unaware of his strength. His control had been so intense that Grace no longer thought of it as lovemaking. More like violation. Her desperation consumed her.

After first arriving at Tullagulla, her shoulder had

taken more than two weeks for the bruising to subside. Now she felt sick and unsure. What was she doing wrong? Why was he so upset with her all the time? Not just her—with everyone? Her guilt and anxiety to do the right thing for him were becoming overwhelming. Picking up the empty scrap bucket, she called to Daniel, determined to put her fears aside and enjoy her life as best she could anyway. "Come on, little man. Do you want to carry the eggs?"

Filled with responsibility and self-importance, Daniel carried the egg bucket carefully, taking one step at a time as he gazed at his precious cargo, trying hard to not let the bucket swing.

"Thanks, mate. You're a real helper."

The little boy beamed lovingly at his mother.

Hastily removing the cake from the oven, Grace replaced it with the apple pie, hoping that his favourite dessert would cheer Pete up. She gave the slow-cooker a stir and turned it down to low, grateful for Beth's tips. At last she was becoming more competent, and she was even managing the old wood stove quite well, considering.

Wanting a sign of inclusion and appreciation from Pete, Grace had been baking and preparing meals for days. She'd also cleaned the master suite for Tom. And each day she'd taken Min and Jarrah out for a ride, with Daniel perched in front of her in the saddle, their crash helmets buckled firmly under their chins.

Pete and Greg were still repairing fences, while Squire had been ordered to check and repair water troughs and bore lines now that there was some water to pump. Grace accepted that there had always been a pecking order in years gone by—a legacy of British rule and squattocracy. In Tullagulla's case, it was Squire who was the most easy-going. He didn't seem to mind that he was ordered around, but her blood still boiled at the unfairness with which Pete treated him. Even calling him Squire instead of Joe annoyed her. *It's derogatory*. The Australian way of giving nicknames was one puzzle that she'd never quite agreed with. However, that issue had been discussed and Grace accepted Squire's decision.

As Daniel chatted randomly to Grace, her mind drifted to Beth—thankful for her friendship and mentoring, and her great care of her son. She was proving to be such a wonderful substitute grandmother, making life on Tullagulla easier for Grace. Daniel loved Beth, and the feeling was obviously mutual. Greg had recently purchased a small electric piano for Beth, her dream since moving to Tullagulla. Now she and Daniel played the piano—or rather, Beth played and Daniel thumped—and Beth sang, encouraging Daniel to sing and dance. Grace had heard him singing about the "Crocodile Wok" and smiled to herself, acknowledging his attempt at Elton John's "Crocodile Rock".

Pete had asked Squire to help him build a sandpit for Daniel under the cedar tree, delighting both Daniel and Grace. During the rare, close, family-oriented week, Grace moved an old cane chair from the side veranda and relocated it next to the sandpit where she could enjoy the peace and tranquillity not always achievable inside the homestead. Not to mention the perfect view down to the airstrip that it gave her. They'd bought some plastic buckets and spades when in town and found an old set of rusty biscuit cutters in the bottom kitchen drawer to make sand cookies with.

Their first winter on Tullagulla was here and with the cold, the risk of snakes reduced, allowing the sandpit to become Daniel's favourite spot to play. Grace could see it through the louvred windows of the corridor while she worked in the kitchen or office, and Min would sit quietly next to Daniel, trailing around the yard after him as he played. Since watching the 'dozer clean out the dams, an old toy bulldozer of Greg's had found its way to Daniel and now spent endless hours rearranging the sand in the sandpit, with the little boy in control.

Grace's attention reverted to the kitchen and she rechecked her list while she watched Daniel talk to Min.

Cooking, done; stock fridge and pantry, done; washing up to date, done; animal feed, enough to last until after shearing, done; child-minding sorted for Daniel, done.

Right, no reason why I can't help, at least with mustering and yarding. Drawing a deep breath, she re-tied her straight, strawberry-blonde hair into a ponytail and pulled on her boots. There was an element of danger in upsetting Pete but as a wave of strength flowed through her body, she knew it was worth the risk.

"Come on, Daniel," she called. "We're going for a ride on the quad bike."

Of all the new deliveries Tom had arranged for Tullagulla, Daniel and Grace's favourite was the quad bike, with Daniel being quick to don his crash helmet and sit in front of his mum at every opportunity. Two quad bikes had arrived on the truck, together with a standard two-wheel farm motorbike. In a few short weeks, the residents of Tullagulla had been wondering how they'd ever managed without them. The big television in the lounge was everyone's second favourite, with Greg and Beth delivered a slightly smaller version. Squire had reassured Tom that a television would not be necessary in his case, in spite of everyone's encouragement.

Grace pulled up outside the woolshed, switched off the bike, and removed their helmets, dropping them in the front basket before lifting Daniel onto the loading dock. A motor was humming deep in the back of the shed, sporadic grinding suggesting the sharpening of shearing combs. Grace glimpsed sparks flying as men's voices shouted to each other over the noise.

She yelled out. "Hello."

Two shearers poked their heads out from a back room, grinning with delight.

"Well, hello, little lady. You make a pleasant change for this shed." The older of the two spoke first. "I'm Bob, and this is Terry." With a flick of his head, he indicated the wiry younger man facing the grinder.

"Hi, I'm Grace, and this is my son, Daniel." Suddenly shy and awkward, her gaze dropped to her boots as the heat crept up her cheeks.

Sensing someone behind her, she whipped around. "Ben!"

"Grace? Fancy meeting you here."

Bob's gaze swung between Grace and Ben. "Am I missing something? Care to explain?"

Ben laughed as he gave Grace a hug. "Grace and I studied wool classing together. She was the best in the class. Flogged the rest of us."

"You're just being nice. I enjoyed it and it was a coincidence that my results were good. How come you're here? I thought you were a true-blue New South Welshman?"

"Well, that's pretty obvious I think. More to the point, what brings you to this shed, Grace? And who is this cute little fellow?" Ben reached out and touched Daniel on the head as he gave him a friendly wink.

"This is my son, Daniel. My husband and I now live here on Tullagulla. My husband, Pete, is the manager."

"Wow, it only seems like last week that we were still at uni. It's great to see you again. I'm married as well now, and we have a little girl about Daniel's age."

Grace relaxed under the glow of Ben's warm smile. It was good to see an old friend.

Ben continued, "Actually, my being here wasn't planned. Old Des, the regular contractor/wool-classer in this team, is crook and rang me to ask if I could help them out. I didn't have much on over the next few weeks and felt like a change of scenery—so here I am."

"Oh, it's so good to see you again." Grace glanced at Daniel, conscious that he had also brightened up, relaxing as he swung back and forth, hanging onto her arm. His shyness usually meant he took most of a visit to someone's place to thaw out and start talking and playing, and by then it was time to leave again. But as he had been with Tom, he seemed comfortable with these three men.

All five of them jumped as Pete's voice boomed over the shed noise.

"Get outside, dog," he spat. Glaring at Grace, his eyes were cold and hard. "You know the rules—no dogs in the shed."

Min had obviously followed Grace inside, laying quietly against the wool press, unseen by all except Pete.

"I didn't realise she had come in. Come on, Daniel. We'd better go." Calling Min to her, she grabbed Daniel and slunk back to the loading dock, furious with herself for not tying Min to the back of the quad bike.

Why is it that he always sees the negatives and catches me out? He's never around when everything is going well, but as soon as I make a mistake, he's right there. She felt like a naughty five-year-old.

Glancing back towards the men as she stepped out into the sun, Ben's face, frozen with shock, caught Grace's eye and her stomach knotted in anguish.

Grace's fingers fumbled as she struggled to fasten Daniel's helmet and the men melted away to find a job to do, seemingly galvanised into action by the changed atmosphere inside the shed. Clutching Daniel tightly in front of her, she accelerated back to the homestead, fuelled by anger and humiliation.

Refusing to stress about her unpredictable husband, Grace operated on autopilot—bathing Daniel and preparing dinner for the family. With no sign of Pete by Daniel's bedtime, Grace tucked him into bed and lay next to him, opening his favourite book. He knew every word by heart and recited bits of *The Gruffalo* with her.

As they turned the last page, he looked up at her. "Why does the lady in the long dress call me David, Mummy? My name is Daniel."

Grace froze, her mind reminiscent of a startled deer in flight. Taking a deep breath, she stammered, "Wh … what lady, Daniel?"

"The lady that sometimes visits me when I go to bed. She whispers but I can't touch her?" He puzzled.

Thoughts, answers, and reason tumbled around in

her head. Daniel stared at her, waiting for her response. *What can I say without frightening him?* "Oh, she's the sleep fairy who visits us when we are really tired. When you see or feel her, you just need to close your eyes and smile, and she will go away and let you nod off."

Daniel smiled his acceptance and snuggled down under the blankets. "She knows when it's just you and me."

"You and I, darling, not you and me," she corrected automatically. *I sound just like my mother.*

Whispering to Daniel as she kissed him goodnight, she said, "The lady is our secret, Daniel."

Who knew what would happen if Daniel mentioned the lady in front of Pete. He would probably dismiss Daniel as being stupid and over-imaginative, but she had no doubt that it would trigger another explosion of temper.

It was nine o'clock in the evening when the kitchen screen door crashed open. Daniel was asleep, Pete's dinner was covered, ready to be heated, and Grace was curled up on the kitchen couch. The television droned in the background, some soap opera drama unfolding as Grace chewed her lip and tried to focus on the screen, a hollow emptiness consuming her mind and body. At the noise, she leapt to her feet, filled with dread, bile rising in her gut.

"I'm starving. Where's my dinner?" he demanded.

Recoiling from the alcoholic fumes, Grace froze as he bent and kissed her.

She reached for his meal, before putting it in the microwave and hitting the start button. "A little celebration to kick off the shearing, I gather?" Grace kept her voice light, forcing a smile on her face as she spoke.

"Yep, all ready and everyone's happy. They've got a good cook too but I thought I'd better not eat with them."

"Righto." Grace nodded, silently praying for a peaceful start to the shearing. It would make a huge difference if everyone was in good spirits in the morning.

"I made apple pie for dessert," Grace announced, plonking the reheated meal in front of him.

Seemingly oblivious to her tension, he grinned at her and, picking up his knife and fork, proceeded to shovel his dinner into his mouth as if he hadn't eaten in a week.

Grace washed and dried the dishes and prepared for bed, by which time Pete was showered and fast asleep, sprawled across three quarters of the mattress.

After lifting up the covers, she slid in beside him and lay staring at the ceiling.

A loud male snore jolted her to the present. Rolling on her side, she turned her back to Pete, resolving again to find out more about the history of Tullagulla and who had lived in this house. Her breath caught as a sliver of concern gripped her stomach. *Should she be afraid for Daniel?*

CHAPTER 15

*T*he cold wind continued to blow as the first week of shearing got underway and the Cessna wobbled wildly as Tom brought it onto the airstrip. Grace's mood climbed rapidly out of the doldrums and she swooped Daniel up and ran outside to the quad bike. As they sped down the track to the airstrip, Tom stepped out of the plane before turning to haul his bag behind him.

"Hi. We're the pick-up crew." Grace laughed as Tom dropped his bag on the rack at the back and swung his leg over the bike behind her.

Grinning, he jammed his Akubra hat hard on his head. "Am I safe? I might have to hold on tight to you." He kept his voice light, but Grace sensed it was full of meaning.

Embarrassed and confused, she turned the bike homeward and drove at a much steadier pace back up the rise, relieved that Tom made no attempt to wrap his arm around her waist.

"So how's it all going?" Tom asked. His warm breath on her neck and the spicy drift of aftershave sent quivers through her as he leaned close to her ear.

"So far, so good." Grace turned her head slightly as she spoke, trying desperately to concentrate on driving the bike safely, not to mention preventing them all from falling off.

While Tom changed his clothes, Grace made a pot of tea and buttered the scones fresh out of Beth's oven this morning.

"Oh, yum. They smell delicious."

Grace smiled, relaxing as Tom's contagious excitement and appreciation spread through her.

"Let's eat up then, and afterwards get you down to the shed so you can meet the crew."

Thankfully, Pete had soon realised that he was short-staffed and had asked Grace for help. Most of the time he seemed appreciative of her contribution, and apart from a couple of abusive tirades, was his old self —even giving her a random hug or a kiss when she least expected it. Though she'd noted wryly that his unexpected display of affection only seemed to happen when one of the men were around and certainly never when the two female roustabouts were watching.

Squire had brought the first mob of sheep in the day before the shearers turned up, filling the pens and pushing the remainder into the yards under the corrugated iron roof. They all understood the importance of keeping them dry and allowing their bellies to empty for everyone's comfort, including the sheep's, before the process of being shorn began. Although rain was unlikely at this time of year, even a heavy dew could affect the moisture in the wool, holding up the shearing. And with the amount of organisation required, no one wanted that.

Mesmerised, Daniel sat on a wool bale watching the buzz of activity while Tom introduced himself to Ben and each of the team as they paused between sheep.

The four shearers bent over their sheep, skilfully sitting each on its tail, their backs nestled firmly against the shearer's legs before picking up the hand-pieces and pulling the cords to engage the electricity. Deftly sweeping the hand-piece under the belly wool, the shearer then flipped it to the side, allowing the roustabout to snatch it away with the broom. The belly was closely followed by the short fluffy wool around the sheep's face and ears, and then the stained section from the rear end. Throwing the pieces into the respective bins, the two roustabouts moved rapidly back and forth across the board, repeating the process while the shearer turned his sheep and plunged the shears into the soft long fleece.

With each swoop of the hand-piece from bottom to top, the perfectly white underside of the wool was exposed as it peeled away from the skin, leaving a fine protective layer on the sheep's body. Scooting their feet under the mound of fleece on the floor, the women bent to pick it up before throwing it high in the air above the slatted wool table, creating a parachute-like landing.

As they turned to the next shearer, Ben dived into the freshly thrown fleece, rapidly spinning the pivoting table as he worked. Prising away the stains, matted pieces of wool, and vegetable matter, he plucked a sample from the shoulder—the most valuable section of the main fleece. Ascertaining its strength and micron, or thickness, he bundled the fleece and threw it into the correct bin.

"Have a look at this, Tom." Ben held a piece of wool up to the shaft of sunlight coming through the window, spreading it open like a cobweb. "In spite of the weather, it's pretty good so far. At least there's no break in the wool, so it should be a good clip."

"What do you mean by a break?"

Ben showed no surprise at the question and smiled, clearly appreciating that Tom was genuinely interested and not afraid of asking about things he didn't know.

"It's a line of weakness in the wool due to stress or a change in feed for the sheep. It drops the value of your wool significantly, as the staple is much shorter which doesn't bring the best money. Luckily you're shearing now. That rain you got recently would have changed the quantity and quality of the feed, and had you waited a couple more months before shearing, we would possibly have seen a break close to the skin."

Tom nodded, his eyebrows raised as he absorbed the young man's knowledge.

Watching as each bin filled, Grace's eyes followed

the presser dashing back and forth and gathering armfuls of fleeces before dumping them into the electronic pressing machine. As soon as the deep, square bin was full, he punched the button—the hydraulic arms lifted the plate into the air before coming down to press the wool into a tight bale bag. It was clipped closed and labelled, the presser running the roller of black ink over the stencils detailing the property name and wool classer's identification, together with the content code.

Each freshly shorn sheep was stood back on its feet before being dismissed through the chute and out into the pen. Grace and the presser took turns to refill the catching pens for the shearers as the outside yards filled up and the shorn sheep were counted. Pete and Ben noted the numbers in the tally book and on the iPad before releasing them into the drafting lane for Squire and Greg to treat them for worms and lice.

The big yard was full of ewes. Grace was concerned that a large number of them were very close to lambing as she saddled Jarrah in readiness for moving them back to the paddock. "You poor girls." Grace's own breast tightened at the full udders. "Of course, the boys have had a free rein and made the most of it with all the broken fences, haven't they? So now you girls have to lamb in the cold and struggle to rear your babies."

Returning to the shed, she was surprised to find Tom holding Daniel, laughing and talking with him as they watched the activity. Pete was penning up more sheep and her hopes rose a little as Tom came towards her. "Don't worry about this little man. I've got him and I'll look after him while you take those sheep back to their paddock. If I get too busy, I'll run him up to Beth's. Won't I, mate?" He tipped him backwards as he tickled his tummy, the excited giggling and flailing of legs sending an avalanche of relief through Grace.

"Thanks heaps, Tom. You're a gem."

Tom winked, grinning at her before turning back towards Pete and the activity. "I reckon Pete just might be a bit too busy to think about him."

Grace smiled, her face an emotional blank canvas in case Pete was watching. She gave Daniel a hug and a little wave before walking out into the bright sunlight.

Trailing the ewes along at a gentle walk as they stopped to snatch mouthfuls of grass, Grace sang softly, her mind a whirl of thoughts and emotions. When they reached the paddock, the sheep flowed through the open gateway, fanning out like a river in flood before spreading across the land, hungry for the shock of green grass that now covered the previously parched earth. Grace checked the trough was full before walking Jarrah around the perimeter. She stopped briefly in the dry stream bed that ran through one side, shaded by huge eucalypts and the occasional large rock and let Jarrah pick a mouthful of the sweet new grass. The heavy rain of a few weeks prior, had been soaked up by the thirsty earth.

Impressed with the new high secure fences, she spoke aloud. "This is a lovely paddock for the new mothers." Min looked at her quizzically.

"Come on then, girl. Time to head back and see what's happening." She latched the gate behind her and kicked Jarrah into a canter towards the shearing shed, Min loping along at her side.

By the time they reached the yards, the days shearing was finished, the shed silent except for the occasional bleat from the sheep penned ready for tomorrow's shearing.

With darkness closing in, the temperature had dropped significantly and Grace struggled to unsaddle Jarrah, her fingers and toes numb with cold. Anxious for her feed, Jarrah nudged her gently.

"You're a good girl," Grace whispered in her ear before she gave her a last rub and left, closing the horse yard behind her. Under the lights of the shearer's quarters, laughter spilled out as the men and women, no doubt freshly showered now, enjoyed a pre-dinner drink.

"Everything okay?"

Grace leapt, clutching the front of her jacket as Tom's concerned voice penetrated the darkness.

"Oh, Tom. You gave me a fright." She laughed. "Yes, all okay. I was just thinking about the ewes. I hope the foxes can't get through the new fence and take the lambs."

"Hmm, we'll check with Squire. He said he's been getting a few foxes so he'll know what the danger is likely to be for them."

Grateful for his empathy, Grace's thoughts were

still with the sheep and she missed the start of Tom's next enquiry.

"… being a wool classer?"

"Sorry. What did you say?"

"I said you never mentioned that you are a wool classer? And I believe it's you who has the agricultural degree, not Pete?"

Grace froze, confused. "I-I-I didn't realise that you didn't know that? Pete said I wasn't to mention that I've studied wool classing in case I upset anyone or made them think I am undermining their authority. I'm sorry about the misunderstanding." Peering into the dark, Grace strained to gauge Tom's expression, her heart beating rapidly as it plummeted towards her boots.

"Hmm, everything's falling into place now. I must admit, I was struggling to comprehend some of the stuff Pete has said or rather, hasn't said, because I did think he should know more than he seems to, especially regarding the sheep."

"I'm really sorry, Tom. I didn't know that. I would never lie to you." Grace paled, nausea burning the back of her throat at the deception under which Pete had acquired his position of manager. The sudden possibility of them being asked to leave Tullagulla overwhelmed her, despair slowing her step and plunging her into misery.

"Daniel's with Beth and Greg. I thought it would be dark by the time you got back so decided that was best?" Tom explained as they walked towards the house, his voice filled with concern. He continued, "Don't worry, Grace. I'm not annoyed or disappointed with you." His voice was gentle as he spoke. "Actually, it's great to meet a woman who's so honest and capable. After my divorce, I didn't think I was much good at reading women, but maybe I'm not so bad after all?"

Grace started at the mention of his divorce, then smiled wanly at him. "Thanks, Tom. I'll just go and collect Daniel. I gather Pete's over at the shearers' quarters again?"

Tom nodded, his mouth clamped shut. Grace smiled ruefully. *Hmm, I thought so. He seems rather taken by that shapely brunette roustabout. Better watch out though —one of the shearers is her husband.*

Pushing open Beth's door, Grace called out and was greeted by the delicious smell of dinner cooking and an excited little boy thumping down the hall towards her, his arms outstretched. Snatching him up, Grace kicked off her boots as Beth's smiling face peered around the kitchen door.

"How was your day?" Beth asked as she wiped her hands on the tea towel.

"Good thanks, Beth. I think we might have a few early lambs in the yards before we get the shearing finished though."

Beth's face dropped. They both knew that any ewes who lambed in the yards would be unlikely to mother them. The stress on them was simply too great.

"Well, let's just see what tomorrow brings, heh? I've been over with my little mate and stoked up the fire for you. I might dig out my lamb bottles and teats just in case?"

"Oh, you're a darling, Beth. What would I do without you?"

Beth waved the tea towel dismissively as she smiled. "Oh, you do go on. Off you go. Drop my little mate back in the morning if you like? We'll come for a walk down to the shed for a while, but it's too much for him to be there all day."

"Okay. See you in the morning then." Grace helped Daniel put his boots on and they waved goodbye to Beth before skipping back to the homestead, holding hands and giggling as they went. She hoped Pete stayed down at the shearers' quarters again so she could enjoy a peaceful evening with Tom.

Unfortunately, that wasn't to be. His voice boomed down the corridor as she stepped out of the shower. Her intense disappointment surprised her.

Three weeks later, shearing was over, the sheep returned to the newly fenced paddocks, and the woolshed floor stacked high with pressed bales of fine merino wool. They had come through their first shearing, Ben had confirmed the clip was good, and Grace was relieved that Pete had mostly kept his cool and not abused anyone. *Well, no more than was usual, anyway.*

Since Tom's mention of his divorce, Grace had been intrigued, bursting to ask him more. *I wonder what sort of woman she was. How come it didn't work out between them?*

Grace waited to see if he would open up and tell her about his ex-wife. However, they didn't get another chance to be alone and no more was said. She didn't dare cross the boundaries and upset Pete. Once again, her heart was heavy as she waved the Cessna away into the sparkling blue winter skies over Tullagulla.

CHAPTER 16

It's hard to believe we've only been here for a few months.

Tullagulla now felt like home except for one thing. She was lonely. Grateful for the older woman's friendship and support, she and Daniel both loved Beth. However Grace missed having a friend of her own age living close by and she was sure Daniel felt the same.

Pete should be my friend. The knowledge that her relationship with Pete was neither a friendship or love any more, if it ever had been, created panic and despair deep inside.

How had the descent of their relationship happened? She questioned herself regularly. Had it just been lust, and never love? Not knowing what to do about it, she took each day as it came and refused to think about the future. Reminding herself that Georgie was only a phone call away, she resolved to ring her more regularly.

At seven o'clock every Sunday night, like clock-work, Grace's parents rang the Tullagulla landline for a chat. Grace looked forward to her weekly family catch-up and if Daniel was still awake, he was allowed the first five minutes to talk to Nanny and Poppy.

This Sunday was no different. Pete answered the phone while Grace washed the dishes and tidied the kitchen.

"Tullagulla," he mumbled. Pausing, he then said, "Hi. Yep, she's here."

He handed the phone to Grace and sat in the kitchen, his back to the office, listening to her conversation.

As she hung up, Pete turned and caught her eye, his forehead set in a deep frown and his eyes glazed with anger. Grace's stomach clenched and her lip quivered, unsure of what she had done wrong this time.

"These conversations with your family are ridicu-lous. You don't need to tell them what is happening here. What goes on is our business and has nothing to do with anyone else."

Grace's feet were glued to the floor as she struggled to process Pete's reaction. "W-what are you talking about? They just want to chat to me. It's quite normal, you know, for parents to talk to their children reason-ably regularly, especially when we live eight hours' drive from them. It's also normal to tell them what we do out here. They're interested and are not being nosey." Her stomach flip-flopped with anxiety as her legs propelled her across the floor towards the bedroom. Slamming the door behind her, she bit her lip, hot tears trickling down her face.

Why is he doing this to me? Is it my fault? Her head full of doubts and questions, she stumbled to the shower and absentmindedly stared at her shaking hand as she reached to turn on the taps.

After stripping off her clothes, she stepped under the stream of water, her face crumpling. Tipping her head back, she let the warmth run over her, washing her tears down the drain together with her hopes. She had been so madly in love in the beginning—she couldn't fault him. His charm, generosity, and tenderness had reassured Grace that he was the one. Thinking about it now, she bitterly chided herself for rushing in and not spending more time together before she made the commitment of marriage. She knew him being away at the mines hadn't helped either. He'd rarely been at home for any longer than a few days and she and Daniel had made the most of his company when he was with them—forgiving and excusing any bad-tempered outbursts as the result of having to work such long and tiring hours.

Pete's heavy footsteps thudded into the lounge and she stiffened, expecting him to barge into the bathroom and rant at her. However, the slam of the bar fridge followed by the clink of the rum bottle against glass confirmed his intentions and she ruefully speculated what was best—Pete drinking too much, or his abuse—or did they go hand in hand?

The sound of the football on television drowned out any further chance of discussion and Grace silently crossed the room towards their bedroom. Pete had his back to her as he sprawled on the couch, a glass in hand. His hair was overdue for cutting and the two-week growth on his chin gave him a rougher look than usual. Climbing into bed, despair washed over her as she pulled up the doona and hunkered down in a heap of misery.

Waking with a start, her body stiffened. *There it is again —someone is definitely walking back and forth outside Daniel's bedroom. I am not imagining it. Is it Pete?*

As she slid her feet onto the floor, she glanced at the lump on the other side of the bed. Then she stood for a minute, reassuring herself that it was Pete and he was fast asleep.

Opening the door just enough to peep out, she listened again for the soft sweep of fabric on the old timber floor. Her nerves as taut as wire, she studied the room. No one was there. A breeze fluttered through the open door from the veranda and the curtain rustled slightly, as subtle as a leaf falling from the tree.

Uncertain how the door had opened, she pulled it closed, shivering as she checked the latch was in place before tiptoeing over to Daniel's room. He was still sleeping soundly, clutching his raggedy toy rabbit.

Carefully and gently, she climbed back into their bed, her mind now wide awake and buzzing, her nerves on fire.

I know someone was there. Checking on Daniel? But who and why? It was nearly four a.m. and there would be no more sleep for her.

"You're up early this morning?" Pete's comment barely registered as she raised her eyebrows.

"Check the clock—I'm no earlier than usual. Do you want scrambled or fried eggs this morning?"

"Scrambled. Coffee brewed?"

"Of course." Grace was short with him as she struggled to contain her frustration. His observations of the morning routine never seemed to improve. She was out of bed before him every day and unless it had been prearranged, breakfast was at six-thirty.

After eating, Pete pushed his chair and arched his back, announcing, "Need you to go to town for parts. I ordered them on Monday and they said they'll be arriving today on the ten o'clock truck."

"Sure. I need to do a few things anyway so that'll work."

"What else do you need to do?"

"Groceries, and I want to get a birthday card for Mum and maybe get my hair cut?"

He shrugged dismissively. "Whatever. See ya later then." Slamming the screen door behind him, he sat on the porch step to pull on his boots before turning slightly, calling out, "Make sure you buy ice cream and more toffees."

Grace rolled her eyes. "Will do. I'll leave a plate of lunch in the cold room for you."

She checked that he had disappeared under the honeysuckle, then raced around the kitchen, hastily packing Daniel a lunchbox—firing into it sandwiches, fruit, muesli bars, and enough water to get them both through the day. Glancing at the clock, she chewed her lip. The supermarket wasn't open yet, and Daniel was still asleep. *Okay, now me.*

By the time Daniel called out to her, his voice still drowsy, she was dressed and ready for a day in town. The car fridge was switched to chill, chooks fed, and washing on the line. After helping Daniel drag his favourite polo shirt and jeans on as he ate his breakfast, the little boy chattering excitedly, she tied the laces on his *Paw Patrol* sneakers and dialled the supermarket.

Too late for an online grocery order today, she breathed a sigh of relief when the cheery girl at the end of the line agreed to take a phone order for her.

That will save me at least half an hour. Haircut might not happen today either—too little notice. She smiled as she washed and dried the last of the breakfast dishes, and helped Daniel reach his 'going to town' cowboy hat.

Driving out over the grid, she straightened her shoulders and let a wave of joy slowly spread through her body. *We're free for the day.* Grinning, her mind ran through her plans. After pressing the start button for the CD player, she welcomed the upbeat strumming of the Zac Brown Band and the sound of waves crashing. *"Knee Deep". Perfect. Her smile widened as she settled into the two-hour drive.*

As the grain silos appeared ahead, the road widened slightly and houses and sheds replaced the she-oaks and belah.

Grace's mind ran in dot points:

- Transport depot first; pick up parts (very important)
- Newsagent for Mum's card
- Post office and bank
- Pick up groceries
- Visit Henry

Pulling into the transport depot, Grace muttered a quiet prayer. "Please don't let them spend half the day looking for our order."

The woman behind the counter didn't make eye contact as Grace stood in front of her. *Perhaps she's deaf?* Grace cleared her throat before speaking. "Excuse me. I've come to collect parts that were ordered for Tullagulla."

In slow motion, the woman turned and stared at Grace with a face sour enough to curdle milk. She slid a box along the counter and gave a loud, wet sniff.

"Thank you." Grace grinned at her before turning and walking back to the car, pleased to have escaped without conversation.

I wonder what's ruined her day—or is she always like that?

"Town's pretty quiet today." She spoke aloud as she angle-parked in the wide, main street. Glancing at her watch, she slung her handbag over her shoulder, locked the vehicle, and took Daniel by the hand as they headed up the street, a smile plastered on both their faces.

Three hours later, they ate their lunch at the park as Daniel ran back and forth between the swings and climbing equipment. Then, with errands completed and the back of the car loaded with groceries and machinery parts, Grace put the LandCruiser into gear and headed out of town.

"Hi, Henry."

The brown, crinkled face of the old gentleman looked up, his surprisingly blue eyes watering with pleasure as a wide smile stretched across his face. "Ooh you're a sight for sore eyes, you two. Come away inside. Perfect timing for a hot chocolate hey, little man." Patting Daniel on the head, he lay his digging fork against the fence before rubbing his back, his stiff gait leading the way back towards the cottage. Pushing open the back door, he turned and smiled again before holding the door open as he gave a shallow bow of delight.

Having devoured their hot drinks and a plate of biscuits, Henry and Grace still sat at the tiny table as Daniel followed Pansy outside into the sunshine.

As soon as he was out of earshot, Grace blurted, "Do you believe in ghosts, Henry?"

"Well. I guess I probably do?" It was a drawling question more than an answer. "What makes you ask?"

"I think there's a ghost at Tullagulla."

Henry stretched back into his seat, a rueful smile spreading over his face. "I've no doubt there would be at least one, lass. It's got a history, even if no one is really sure what that is."

"So, do you believe in ghosts?"

"Weeell, yes. At least, I believe the presence of a past resident is sometimes reluctant to leave. Tell me more?"

Grace quietly poured out her experiences and the sensations she'd felt, including the comments Daniel had made about the lady in the long skirt.

Henry sat perfectly still, absorbing every word Grace said, contemplative as he rubbed his chin before he responded. "From what you've just told me, I wonder if it could be Angus's wife. She lived there in the days when long dresses were the normal daily attire and must have had a child at some point—and obviously they both passed on. Maybe she is just visiting you and Daniel because you're the first woman and child in the house since she died. It seems that she hasn't made her presence known to any men living there. Jock would have mentioned it to me if he'd felt anything. He was a kind and sensitive soul." A wave of sadness appeared to engulf him as he spoke thought-fully, almost apologetic that he couldn't give Grace a more informative response.

"Daniel said the lady called him David. I wonder if that was Angus' child's name?"

"That might not be too difficult to find out. Perhaps one of those ancestry thingys might help?"

"Hmmm. Maybe." Grace stared into her mug, as if expecting an answer to launch itself from the bottom of the vessel. "Thanks for listening anyway. At least you don't think I have a mental illness." She smiled as her mouth twisted.

"Of course not. Every time you feel a presence, why don't you make a little note, in your diary or on that fancy phone you young ones carry around with you, and see if it coincides with anything specific that may be happening in the house? Maybe she only appears in certain weather, or if the mood in the house causes her concern."

His last comment startled Grace and she jerked her head up to study his face, which was even more creased now than before. Recognising a deep wisdom in his rheumy eyes, panic filled her, her chair almost toppling backwards as she jumped to her feet. Surely he couldn't know about how Pete treated her? Embarrassment flooded her body as heat crept up her neck.

With perfect timing, Daniel burst into the room again, breaking the spell. "Can I have a carrot please?"

They both laughed, Henry pushing his hands on the table as he struggled to his feet. "Come on then, young fella. Let's pull up a couple and see if they are big enough."

Grace smiled at her son. "Okay. Then we had better

get off home before the ice cream melts. Thanks for the drink and chat. We'll call in and see you again next time if that's okay?"

"Of course. Remember what I said. Take notes!"

Grace gave a salute, giggling as she picked up her bag and slung it over her shoulder. She blinked in the bright winter sunlight as they stepped outside.

CHAPTER 17

The familiar buzz of the approaching Cessna increased, like a frustrated blowfly trapped against the window, and Grace scanned the sky, a warm glow flushing her cheeks. Tom rocked the wings in greeting as he caught sight of her and Daniel in the house yard.

They had six newborn lambs in a pen under the cedar tree. She had been right—several ewes had lambed early, and in the stress and confusion of being yarded, six ewes had refused to care for their babies. Grace mixed up artificial colostrum for them and she and Daniel were feeding them several times a day now on powdered milk formula. All male lambs, they would be kept as wool growers, delighting both Daniel and Grace—who was relieved they were merinos and not a breed grown for meat.

The ute clattered past the house yard, headed towards the plane, making its way along the slope to the flat where the windsock hung limply in the bright winter sunshine. Since the plumbago hedge had been given a good haircut, the airstrip was much more visible to the house. And on the days Tom was expected to arrive, both Grace and Daniel hovered around the veranda and sandpit as much as possible.

After gathering up the empty lamb bottles, Grace stacked them in the bucket and called to Daniel, "I'm going inside now to put the kettle on. Are you coming?"

"No, I'm busy," Daniel retorted as he pushed an old Tonka truck, courtesy of Beth, through the sandpit without raising his head.

Grace laughed. "Okay. See you inside when you are ready."

Turning her head, she checked that Min had stayed with him and not followed her to her favourite spot on the step. She was such a good little guard dog. Laying on the edge of the sandpit, letting the winter sun soak into her black coat, her tan eyebrows gave her a quizzical appearance as she watched Daniel from one sleepy eye.

Pete was in a good mood today and Grace breathed a sigh of relief. Her love of Tullagulla was deepening. She enjoyed life here and hated it when Tom had to witness Pete's true colours. Her greatest fear now was that Pete would expose his foul temper once too often in Tom's presence and they'd have to leave.

As the ute door slammed, she filled the teapot with boiling water and carried it to the table. Tom opened the screen door in front of Pete, flooding the room with light as he stepped inside.

Beaming at Grace, he bent and gave her a peck on the cheek and a gentle hug. "How's the Tullagulla missus going then?" he joked.

"As good as the Tullagulla owner I think," Grace quipped, her nostrils filled with the scent of his aftershave.

Pete grinned as he threw his battered Akubra on the hat rack and pulled out a chair. "Tom reckons Tullagulla's flush enough to buy more cattle," he announced.

"Well." Tom started as a crease appeared between his eyebrows. "Financially, things are not as bad as we thought, and although the drought has been tough, I've been doing my research. If we sort out the hotchpotch of cattle that are on this property, we could sell off what isn't doing well here and restock with Droughtmasters. I think they'll do better and will be a good investment."

Pete was excited. He was more of a cattleman than a sheep man. Grace hadn't seen him this animated since they'd moved here. She knew of the chestnut-coloured Droughtmaster breed, developed by crossing Brahman and Shorthorn cattle. They were bred for this type of country and would handle the extreme conditions well.

Tom continued, "I've been doing quite a lot of reading and have also taken advice from an old friend of my father's. He's always had cattle and sheep properties as a sideline to his export business, so I've been picking his brains." He laughed. "Amazing what you learn when you start hunting, and now I have a reason to need to know, I can't get enough of it." He shrugged sheepishly, seemingly embarrassed by this admission.

"I think that's awesome, Tom, and I totally agree. I never had much opportunity to learn about sheep and wool growing up on a dairy farm, but I really love them and I enjoyed helping Dad with our little flock of Dorpers before we moved here. That's probably why I … I studied sheep a bit more when I was at uni …" She trailed off as Pete's stare locked with hers, a conscious reminder of his unspoken annoyance at her revealing information about herself.

Tom's smile widened as he stared at Grace, his understanding of her anxieties complete as he spoke. "Yes, I am beginning to realise how interested you are in farming and stock. Lucky me, scoring a couple with so many qualifications to run my property."

Grace breathed a sigh of relief as Pete smiled, taking Tom's comment as a compliment to him.

"We make a good team really, don't we?" Grace responded quietly.

"So how long are you staying this time, Tom?" Pete asked, ignoring Grace's comment.

"I can spare a few days if that's okay? I wouldn't mind having another look at the cattle and I wondered if maybe we could do another muster of them. Also, I want to organise a truck and get that wool to the wool stores. We really need to sell it sooner rather than later to balance the books."

Pete nodded. "We'll start in the morning if you like?

You and I can take the ute this time, Tom. Grace, you and Squire take the horses and Greg can use the quad bike. I think we'll leave the dogs at home too. We could have our work cut out and the dogs will only upset the cows with calves."

Hours later, Grace finished tidying up the kitchen. Daniel was in bed, and she could hear Tom and Pete talking in the lounge room. Still warm with pleasure, she'd been delighted when Tom had jumped up from the dinner table, offering to help with the dishes. Pete never helped with household chores.

"Leave the dishes, Tom. That's Grace's job. Come through to the lounge and have a drink. The footy's starting in a few minutes."

"Great, thanks, Pete. You go through and pour me a drink. I'll just give Grace a hand." Tom's tone was firm and dismissive and, after a confused stare, Pete accepted his decision and turned towards the lounge without another word.

Grace scraped the plates into the chook bucket and rinsed them quickly under the tap before she put the plug in and allowed the hot soapy water to rise slowly in the sink. Turning to look at Tom, she caught his raised eyebrow, and decided the time was right. "What happened with your relationship, your wife?"

As Grace bit her lip, afraid that she had spoiled their evening, Tom smiled and looked at her thoughtfully before answering. "Not enough in common, I guess. She's a great woman—a fashion editor. We were married for seven years and our separation was amicable. She liked her life in the fashion world and didn't want children. And I, well, I guess I'm the opposite."

Grace smiled tentatively at him as she reached out and removed the tea towel from his hand. "You'll be a great father. Better get into your drink and footy now before we're both in trouble. Thanks for your help." She glanced self-consciously at her dirty jeans and sweaty work shirt with its torn sleeve and paint splashes, surprised at how one man could make her feel so incredibly petite and feminine, and wished she'd had time for a shower and clean clothes before dinner.

Oh well. Such is life. She was unable to prevent her smile from spreading as she did a little twirl into the pantry and back.

I know I'm not pretty, but that man has a way of making me feel quite attractive.

"Not watching the footy with us, Grace?" Tom asked as she crossed the room towards the bathroom.

"I'll just have a shower first and will be right out." She smiled.

After shutting the bathroom door, she leaned back and took a deep breath. A lot had happened since she'd arrived at Tullagulla. *What the hell is happening to me?*

CHAPTER 18

*G*race called the horses and Jarrah nickered in response as she followed her mistress into the stables. Being winter, the horses all got a feed of hay at night and morning, which made catching them for an early start much easier. Squire appeared out of the dark and whistled for Beau to follow him.

"Lucky you—no sore bum for you tonight," she quipped at him.

"Tell you what, we'll take turns. You can ride him next time 'round. Just remember though, it's age before beauty and I'm older than you," he retorted with his lopsided grin and his shy, cultured drawl.

Grace laughed, raising her eyebrows as she threw the saddle on Jarrah's back. Their conversations were lengthening and she enjoyed Squire's company, even if getting anything from him was like squeezing blood from a stone.

Maybe he's just the type that takes a long time to thaw out with people—wise move.

They rode out of the yards as the sun was creeping over the eastern horizon. Beth had arrived at the homestead in the dark to care for Daniel as Grace scraped the last plate of its bacon rind and egg leftovers. Pete and Tom had already driven off and Grace heard the quad bike start up as Beth had opened the kitchen door.

Grace agreed with Tom – the cattle on Tullagulla certainly were a hotchpotch. A mixture of Angus, Herefords, Red Devon, and a few dairy cows. They had interbred far too long, progressively becoming weaker.

However, they all accepted that those that remained were obviously strong enough to have withstood the conditions and had picked up since being drenched. Now they had much better feed thanks to the rain a few weeks ago and Tom's injection of capital and truckloads of hay. Some of the cattle barely resembled their former selves.

"Righto." Squire waved his arm towards Grace, indicating that they drift apart and head back towards the yards, gathering the cattle as they went.

Grace was used to dealing with stock but there was an ocean of difference between these half wild and rarely handled Tullagulla cattle and her parents' lovely dairy herd. "No scratches on the head for you lot," she said out loud. "I'd probably lose my arm." She smiled to herself, humming Lee Kernaghan's "Boys from the Bush" as she trailed behind the mob who alternated between staring at her and Jarrah, and turning tail and galloping ahead. She held the reins in her left hand, her stock whip hung loosely over her right shoulder, the plaited leather handle sitting comfortably in her palm.

She listened as Squire cracked his whip occasionally, his low tones calling quietly to the cattle, "Walk up, walk up. Whoa, boys and girls."

Grace took heed of Squire's example and discovered her initial fearful respect for this mob eased as she talked and sang to them. She only cracked her whip once when an inquisitive steer came too close to her, probably just for a better look, but too close for comfort. "Best you know who's boss here, my lad," she said to him as he held her eye for a moment before turning and fleeing to the rest of the herd.

It was a slow process and mid-afternoon by the time she and Squire sighted the cloud of dust ahead, indicating the cattle yards and action. She was grateful for the sandwich and apple she had put in her saddlebag, although they hadn't stopped so she'd eaten as they rode. The horses had slowed to a sedate walk now, tired after their solid trotting and cantering for the kilometres to the back boundary. However, if asked, both Jarrah and Beau would leap into action should a cattle beast attempt to break away from the mob.

Funnelling into the big yard, the cattle were eager to join their friends up ahead, and Squire called back to Grace to close the gates as he rode ahead and pushed them up into smaller yards.

After swinging her leg over the back of the saddle,

Grace stepped down to the ground, her legs almost buckling underneath her. Surprised, she laughed, glancing around quickly to ensure no one was watching. *How embarrassing. I ride more often than anyone.* She stretched her back and legs as she pushed the heavy iron gates closed and remounted, the circulation tingling now in her thighs and buttocks.

Coughing the thick dust from her throat, she waved the flies from her face and turned to see the ute coming up beside the yards.

"All good?" Pete yelled out of the driver's open window.

"Yep, I think so."

"Okay. You might as well go and unsaddle now. We'll give this lot some hay and let them settle down overnight. Just check that trough over the other side of the yard's full, will ya?"

"Will do." Grace turned wearily, kicking Jarrah into a brisk walk across the hundred-metre-wide yard.

Reaching the trough, she turned back to the ute and gave a thumbs up signal to Pete. Responding with a brief nod, he accelerated away, the cloud of dust in his wake descending over the yards.

"Thanks, Pete. A dust shower is just what I needed right now," Grace muttered, a little surprised at her own sarcasm. Strolling over to the small exit gate on the side fence, she pitched forward suddenly, shock and agony draining the colour from her face as her lower stomach cramped. Holding onto the saddle, she took several deep breaths, waiting for the pain to ease.

Then, latching the gate behind her, she remounted slowly and let Jarrah carry her back to the stables. No point calling for Pete's help as the noise of the bellowing cattle was deafening and no one would even see her through all the dust.

She slid off her horse, her legs collapsing as she hit the stable floor, her head spinning and her body wracked with more painful cramps. She wasn't sure how long she sat there, but at Jarrah's gentle nudge, she struggled to her feet and unsaddled and fed her. Staggering out into the fading sunshine, she was sorry now that she had walked this morning instead of riding the quad bike. She had to shuffle back to the house, the usual ten-minute distance feeling more like an hour.

Thankfully, as she stumbled up the step into the kitchen, Beth and Daniel were nowhere to be seen. Desperately thirsty, Grace reached for a bottle of water from the cold room and hobbled along the hall to the bathroom.

Shutting the door behind her, she stripped off her jeans, her eyes wide with shock as the blood trickled down her legs. Pain coursed through her, but what was causing it? Her blood ran cold. She'd been pregnant. Grace had attributed her erratic moods over the previous few weeks to her anxiety over Pete. She counted back now to when she'd last had a period, flopping against the wall as the truth registered.

Fumbling around in the bathroom cupboard, she found a packet of pads and an old towel she had stored for cleaning. Then she stepped under the flow of warm water. In shock, she sat on the shower floor, the water coursing over her, allowing herself several minutes of rest before the strength seeped back into her legs. She hauled herself onto her feet, turned off the taps, and towelled herself dry before pulling on her clean clothes and stumbling to the bedroom.

Weak and pale, she lay on the bed.

"Just a few minutes." She convinced herself. Drifting in and out of a hazy doze, Grace was vaguely aware of the gentle hand stroking her forehead before the merest whisper of a skirt swished out of the room and she melted into the sleep of the exhausted.

The sound of men's voices startled her into the present. Confused by memories and dreams, she tentatively rolled to the side of the bed before hauling herself to her feet.

Pausing, she took a deep breath and then crept to the door and across the hallway to the bathroom.

"Yes, I'm alright." She spoke to the reflection in the mirror before bending and gathering up the dirty, bloodied clothes and towels. As she negotiated the kitchen steps to the laundry, the gate was thrown open and Pete ducked under the honeysuckle, followed closely by Tom. They were covered in dust with the exception of the skin around their eyes, their sunglasses having provided them both with a comical mask. The defined line across their foreheads, the stamp of a jammed-on Akubra that was not going to blow off anytime soon, perfectly divided the dirt from the clean portion of their heads.

"We'll need you to help again tomorrow," Pete announced to Grace. "You can record the tags. Tom and Squire can push up. I've got Greg on the head bale, and I'll brand and tag anything that's clean."

Grace nodded as she turned into the laundry, throwing the washing into the tub, her face pale and stony. The tags held recorded information and every ear-tagged bovine in Australia had to be scanned and information provided every time they moved location. The National Livestock Identification System, or NLIS, worked well, provided the scanner functioned properly and the details were transferred onto the waybill correctly. If not, there would be a lot of swearing and frustration in the yards tomorrow, and she really wasn't sure she would cope with that.

In the kitchen, at first Grace avoided Tom's gaze as she picked up the cake tin and sugar jar before dumping both unceremoniously on the table and turning to boil the kettle.

After pouring the steaming-hot liquid into the mugs, she lifted her face to meet Tom's steady gaze. Surprised at how his hazel eyes had filled with concern, she touched her forefinger to her lips and subtly gave her head a slight shake.

Pete jumped up from the table as soon as they had finished their drinks and strode into the office, announcing loudly, "I'll just grab that new bag of ear-tags for the cattle that haven't been tagged."

Tom picked up the empty mugs, stacking them on top of one another as he followed Grace to the sink. "Are you okay?" His voice was soft and so kind, Grace almost let her fiercely held tears roll down her face.

"Just a bit tired, and ah, women's stuff."

"Oh, I'm sure we'll manage if you'd rather stay here tomorrow?"

"It's okay, Tom. I feel better now and it's only light work, so I'll be fine. I'm just going to collect Daniel. Help yourself to another cuppa if you like."

She dawdled along the track to Beth's cottage, deep in contemplation. *Funny how the boss notices but my darling husband is totally oblivious.*

Grateful for the later start the next morning, she squeezed into the front seat of the ute, one leg on either side of the gear stick as Pete filled the driver's side with his big frame, and Tom slid into the passenger seat beside her.

She mentally braced for another long, tiring day in spite of her body rebelling. Even though she had tried to pre-prepare meals for these busy times, it seemed that it was always busy. At least she and the dreaded wood fire had finally become friends. It cooked big chunks of meat or chicken so slowly that it fell off the bone and melted in the mouth, provided the wood was the right size and the thermostat stayed in the right place. With Beth's help, a couple of tattered old recipe books, and a few tips from her mum, she had rediscovered recipes from her childhood and revisited her grandmother's delicious-smelling kitchen. She was becoming quite adept at rice and bread and butter puddings, egg custard, and all manner of casseroles and vegetable dishes.

Tom's leg pressed against hers in the cramped cab and with her mind desperate to focus on anything else but their bodies, Grace's breaths were short and shallow. In her effort to distract herself from the physical situation, she forced herself to think about what she would prepare for dinner. There was still enough casserole left over from last night, so she would throw in some potatoes to bake, and steam some beans and carrots. For dessert she could core and stuff a few of those bright green Granny Smith apples in the cold room with dates, brown sugar, and cinnamon. If Pete hadn't raided the freezer without her knowing, there should be enough ice cream to go with the apples.

Another cramp clutched her stomach as she climbed out of the ute and she bent double, her breath catching as she pretended to adjust her boot. What she really wanted to do was to lay down and sob her heart out. Her hormones were haywire and at that moment, she hated her husband. She hadn't even had a chance to talk to him. He was always either preoccupied or disinterested, and the opportunity had not eventuated. She doubted he would even care that she had been pregnant, let alone be concerned for how she was feeling about it.

He needs to know. He's my husband.

With the day progressing in a blur, she operated on autopilot, ignored Pete's bad temper, and was relieved when he dismissed her to go home and prepare dinner.

CHAPTER 19

Tom stayed for several days following the cattle muster—his peaceful, intelligent presence around both the house and property had a positive effect on them all. His interest in everything was stimulating, astounding Grace with his ability to absorb all he heard or saw like a sponge. At times, Pete had not been able to hide his know-it-all attitude and Tom took to quietly asking Grace questions about farming as they continued his riding lessons with Pete nowhere in earshot. Grace was delighted at Tom's natural ability to ride, rising to the trot easily as they squeezed in an hour's riding lesson each afternoon.

Away from the restriction of the yard, they ventured along Tullagulla's tracks, travelling in different directions each day with Tom on Spike, and Grace and Daniel riding Jarrah. Encouraging Tom to take the lead when the track narrowed, Grace was a little embarrassed at the excitement churning her insides as her eyes feasted on his slim, straight back and long strong legs. As she followed him one cold afternoon, the thought of sitting behind him, her arms tucked into his snuggly sheepskin-lined leather vest, sent shivers of desire through her.

Who would have thought? Grace focused on the wide-brimmed Akubra jammed tightly over his curly hair, smiling. Pinching herself, she prised her thoughts away from his body and back to their conversation as she called out to him, "You've completed your first few units in the 'Degree in Tullagulla'. Your next lesson is the cropping unit."

He swung around in the saddle, grinning at Grace as Spike kept on walking, rhythmically rocking Tom's body gently back and forth.

"Once these new Droughtmasters are settled, we need to get ready to harvest," she called.

It wouldn't be a big harvest but they were all pleased Greg had used the brief window of opportunity to prepare the ground and plant about half of what they hoped to achieve in better seasons.

Guilt consumed her. Watching Tom sitting on the floor playing with Daniel after dinner each night brought joy to her and delight to her son. An outsider could have assumed Tom was Daniel's dad.

Tom stared down at her before climbing into the plane and glanced over her head at Daniel sitting happily on the quad bike. "Are you sure you're okay? You're still very pale and I'd love to help if I can?"

"I had a miscarriage on the afternoon of the cattle muster," she blurted. She wasn't sure why she told him. Perhaps it was the compassion he showed, or perhaps it was something deeper?

A changing mix of emotions swept across his face before his mortified stare locked with Grace's solemn one. His eyes glued to Grace's, he pulled out a handkerchief, removed his glasses, and rubbed each lens clean. "Oh, Grace, you shouldn't have come back to the yards with us. You should have been taken to the hospital."

Grace smiled dismissively. "It's all okay, honestly. It was very early days and nothing I couldn't handle. You can close your mouth now," she joked.

Tom grinned, snapping his lips together. "Geez, you're a tough little lady."

"Probably not as tough as any other woman living in the bush, especially these days."

"True. Let me know if you need anything though."

Unspoken thoughts had consumed her mind as, slightly embarrassed, he climbed into the cabin of the little Cessna and put his headset on.

Turning back to Grace, he lifted his hand in farewell, smiling with not just his wide, friendly mouth, but also with his eyes in the familiar way Grace had come to recognise. The plane taxied along the airstrip, turning to face her again, and a warm flood of affection washed over her.

The culled hotchpotch of Tullagulla's cattle herd had been trucked away to the saleyards and for a brief period, life had returned to relative peace and quiet. The men were out along the boundaries again, anxious to complete the new fences, while Grace had been catching up on the backlog of house and office work. Cleaning and de-cobwebbing the windows, giving the stovetop and oven a good scrub, and tidying and reorganising the pantry and cold room had allowed Grace plenty of time to be alone with her thoughts and memories.

She relived Tom's last departure, him dipping the wings of the little aircraft in farewell as the Cessna became a speck in the south-easterly sky heading away from Tullagulla. Grace's tears had flowed freely, torn between her need to recover without Tom's knowing eyes on her, and the emptiness she now experienced when he wasn't around. She missed him more than she should and was riddled with guilt at the realisation that it was Tom she imagined herself with, not Pete.

As Grace slid into bed next to Pete that night, she whispered, "Are you awake?"

A grunt was emitted from under the sheet, and Grace continued, relieved to have the opportunity to talk. Whether Pete listened or not, was another issue.

"You know how I wasn't feeling very well after the cattle muster. Well, I didn't know I had been pregnant, and I lost the baby." She paused, waiting for a reaction. It was slow to come, but Pete rolled onto his back and grunted again.

"Oh. So you're okay now though." It was a statement rather than a question.

"Yes." Grace barely whispered, her despair increasing as Pete turned rolled over and went to sleep.

CHAPTER 20

"*M*um!" Daniel's yell spurred her into a run, arriving at the sandpit in seconds, her blood pumping as she envisaged a brown snake heading straight for her son.

"Look, Mum. The trucks are coming." Daniel was pointing to the approach of three long road trains, the first swinging wide as it approached Tullagulla's entrance.

Relieved there was no snake or spider in sight, Grace shared his excitement, climbing up to the platform above the sandpit. Perfect for a little boy, it had a ladder, a slide coming down, and a steering wheel and gear stick screwed to the wooden railing—enough to be anything he wanted it to be, thanks to Squire. At this moment, it was a great lookout.

The trucks crawled slowly past the house and she glimpsed the white ute taking off from the shed with Pete at the helm, leading the convoy towards the yards.

Bursting with enthusiasm, Daniel begged her to follow them on the quad bike. She hesitated, her uncertainty sparked by the potential of Pete's fury if they got in the way. However, with the pale face anxiously staring at her, filled with hope, she caved and swept Daniel into her arms.

Settling him safely on the seat between her legs, Grace drove the bike slowly to the row of trees near the loading ramp before parking under a casuarina tree, giving them a good view without being too close to the action.

The cattle trucks were unloaded and Grace had supplied everyone with fresh scones and fruit cake with their tea and coffee before the cheery drivers climbed back into their truck cabs and disappeared in a cloud of dust. Pete, Greg, and Squire were consumed with scanning and sorting the cattle, filling the hay feeders with large round bales, and checking the water troughs were functioning properly. They would let them settle for a couple of days before walking them out to the paddocks.

Grace picked up the landline phone and dialled Georgie. It was ages since she had last talked to her friend. Disappointed when the phone went to voicemail, Grace left her message. "Just thought I'd call and catch up. Don't worry about ringing back. I'll try you again when I can."

Driven by unexplained forces, the next day Grace was compelled to clean and tidy the study—a job clearly long overdue. She methodically began with the shelves, dusting and rearranging all the books and diaries in alphabetical and chronological order.

No one had mentioned the tally books since shearing, and Grace had been too busy to give them any thought. As she worked her way down to the bottom shelf, she pulled out an old boot box, fragile and faded. Carefully removing the torn lid, her eyes widened as she unpacked piles of pocket notebooks and shearing records dating from pre-World War II until 2008.

It suddenly dawned on her that the shearing contractor or shed manager probably had the more recent records. She was sorry now that she hadn't asked Ben about them when he was here.

Knowing someone would need the details to not only pay the shearers—they would be paid the regulated amount per sheep—but to also identify each sheep shorn so the information could be used to calculate the amount of wool cut per head and income expected, she convinced herself that the previous contractor must have kept the more recent records. *Maybe Jocks' health wasn't as good as everyone had thought.*

From where she squatted on her haunches, she pushed herself to her feet and carried the box to the kitchen table, pleased that she had found something that Pete would be happy about. She hoped so anyway, and glanced at the clock.

The boys will be home in about an hour. Pete had

radioed through to say he was going to check the bore lines and water troughs. Water was of paramount importance with the temperatures now rising and the arrival of the new cattle. Grace was relieved that at last Pete seemed to be taking more interest in his responsibilities. She crossed her fingers that it lasted.

Turning once again to the study, she focused on the desk and pulled out the top drawer. It was a mess of pens and notebooks, plus a magnifying glass, receipts, and rubbish. The second one seemed to just be full of papers. *Hmm, this is not going to be the quick tidy-up job I hoped.* Losing impetus, she closed it, content to leave it for another day.

Shoving the bottom drawer, Grace struggled to shut it properly. She plonked herself on the floor and pulled it towards her, easing her hand in as she released the overfull pile of documents caught against the one above. Again, it was jam-packed with what appeared to be old farm diaries, exercise books, and piles of receipts bound together with string. Unable to push the drawer back in, she pulled it out fully until it sat on the floor.

As she removed the contents, planning to repack it more tidily, a breeze gusted through the doorway, catching a loose piece of paper. Grace launched herself sideways to grab the airborne scrap, toppling over as she reached out. Landing sharply on her elbow, she yelped and lay on her side. In the seconds she lay there, she caught a glimpse of something white jammed against the framework of the desk. She leapt up and raced to the pantry where she grabbed a torch. Then, lying on her stomach and shining the beam into the cavity, she carefully extracted what appeared to be a tissue-thin piece of letter-writing paper.

Drawing the paper towards her, she noticed another envelope with an old red stamp on it stuck a little farther along the framework. She sucked in a deep breath, gripped the torch between her teeth, and reached into the space again, gently releasing two envelopes from their prison. With widening eyes, she gasped, squinting to read the postmark. The stamp displayed a picture of King George V. She grabbed the magnifying glass and hovered over it, releasing her breath slowly through her teeth. It wasn't her imagination. The envelopes were post-marked 1917.

The clanking of the windmill jogged Grace to attention. Her senses heightened and, not wanting anyone to invade her privacy, she tucked the letters between the top two diaries on the shelf. Tidying up the piles of papers, she stacked them carefully in the corner.

Closing the now-empty drawer carefully and tightly, possibly for the first time in nearly a hundred years, Grace placed her hand on her chest, as though reassuring her pounding heart. Finding the packet of plastic page protectors from the shelf next to the printer, she carefully placed the two envelopes and a single, folded sheet of writing paper inside a sleeve each before running up to the bedroom and tucking them into the bottom of her underwear drawer. She was torn, her pulse racing as her mind fought with her emotions. Desperate to study the letters, she dared not expose her secret to Pete in case he yelled at her for snooping. But she needed to know who they were from, and what they were about. And only then she would know who she could trust enough to share the information with.

With excitement and disbelief mounting, the knowledge of the letters burned into her, distracting her until after lunch the following day when she had a window with enough time alone to revisit them.

Sitting on the bed, Grace carefully prised open the single page. It was so frail she was afraid to touch the fold in case it fell apart. With trembling fingers, she peeled the two halves of the paper away from each other, revealing a faded ink scrawl, once blue or black, but now a wavy, dark cream trail against a white background. Even with the magnifying glass, it was splotched with spots and stains making it difficult to read:

Tullagulla

17 September 1917

My dearest sister Emmy,

I apologise for not replying to your letter before today. I am heartbroken and not myself.

My darling David passed away three days ago from, I believe, influenza. We were unable to reduce his fever and he faded away to be with God.

Angus and his men are away mustering cattle and I do not expect their return for several more days. I could not wait until Angus returned to bury David's little body and even if I could have got a message through to the doctor in town, he would have been too late.

Remember the cedar tree you gave me when we met in Brisbane last year? I had it in a tub where I could give it regular water. It is now three feet high, and after George, (our housemaid's husband) helped me bury David, I planted the tree over his little grave. I trust that in years to come, it will shade and protect my darling son from all weathers.

Again, I apologise, Emmy, for this disjointed letter. I do not feel well and need to lie down. I will continue ...

Anguish gripped Grace. Aching with sympathy, she reread the letter twice as the understanding about why it had ended so abruptly sank in. *The poor, poor lady. So, that was what happened, and that is the lady who calls Daniel, David. I wonder what her name was?*

Grace carefully slid the letter back into the plastic page protector and placed it in the drawer before picking up the envelopes. Both were of similar thickness and as Grace unfolded the contents and laid them side by side on the bed, she was relieved to note the neat, cursive writing was clearer and darker in colour, making reading a little easier. *Perhaps because they have been inside envelopes?*

Hovering the magnifying glass over the first page of each letter, she was just able to make out the dates— one was dated 12 May 1917, and the other 25 August 1917.

Her heart was pounding so loudly that she glanced furtively around as if believing someone might hear it. Trying not to touch the fragile paper any more than she had to, she stumbled over the faint, complicated script, the occasional word indecipherable.

15 Mulgrave Street, Spring Hill, Brisbane

12 May 1917

My dearest sister Jane,

I trust this letter finds you well and happy. David will be a big boy now. Almost three and no doubt good company for you while Angus is away on the property and with business. I can only imagine how much you miss being here in Brisbane with me, as I miss you. However, you are fortunate to have your husband at home, and not still in unknown lands with so many of our brave men.

I regret that we were not able to have a child before Harold's company departed to fight in this dreadful war. However, I am kept busy helping our local church group, baking and knitting for our boys overseas. I have just completed another pair of socks for the next shipment, and can admit to you, I am feeling proud of myself. I unpicked the dark-green-coloured cardigan that I never liked as obtaining wool is difficult at times. I am sure our boys won't mind. It was good quality and the colour quite suitable for socks.

My neighbour, Doreen, has three boys and a husband away fighting and her worries are great. No news from anyone for many months now. So ... I am thankful for my life.

In due course, and God willing, my beloved Harold will return and we will have our own child.

My garden is looking pretty, and I am grateful for the fresh vegetables we can grow in this warm climate. Weren't we fortunate to have a father who taught us well? Not just in our academic studies, but in nature too. Poor Doreen struggles to even grow beans and is pleased to exchange vegetables for fresh eggs and delicious mulberries when her mulberry tree is fruiting.

The cedar tree we admired when you last visited is growing well and now provides beautiful shade over Mr McGuire's front yard. He has placed two chairs under it. He receives so many passers-by who comment and sit awhile. I do hope your tree is growing for you out there? Mr McGuire asked after you yesterday and hopes it brings you happiness.

I am welcoming the cooler weather now. Summers are so dreadfully hot. However, as we both know, the veranda with its lattice shades is a pleasant place to sit. I think of you sitting on your veranda (do you have lattice shades?) as I sip a cool drink and I imagine you doing the same.

Take care of yourself, dear sister, and give David a hug from me.

Until next time, all my love,

Emmy

Grace rubbed her eyes in an attempt to ease the strain, the ache heavy in her heart as she bent her head over the second letter.

15 Mulgrave Street, Spring Hill, Brisbane

25 August 1917

My dearest sister Jane,

I was delighted to receive your letter this week. I understand the vastness of this country and the difficulty in transport, however, I miss you so very much and long for a time when we can see one another more frequently.

How is my beautiful nephew? I do hope he enjoyed his birthday and liked the little jacket I knitted him. He must be a great joy to you and Angus.

I was very relieved to receive a letter recently from Harold. His news is limited but I understand he is in France somewhere by the postmark. He said it is getting quite warm there now, but they live outdoors in tents, so the cold winter will not be welcome. I pray he will return to me soon and this dreadful war will end. He wrote the letter in May, so it has taken three months to reach me.

The hot weather will be upon us again soon, so I am enjoying these cool mornings and the warm kitchen while I can. I know I shouldn't complain, but you know how much I detest the hot weather and the mosquitos that summer brings. I am now revelling in having plentiful hot water and being able to enjoy cooking. Before long, I will be cursing having to light the stove and returning once again to having my face glow with perspiration! Not very lady-like. I wonder how you cope with the weather where you are? It is so nice to be able to write about these things to you. No one else would listen!

I have planted the potatoes, beans, and pumpkins and have been making pickles with the chokos and onions I grew over winter. How fortunate that the choko vine from next door chose to ramble over our shed. Sugar is not always available, however, Mr McGuire's bees have kindly provided me with some honey, and the funny little Chinese man from the fruit shop gave me a spice mix to try. I added some to the pickles as they were cooking and they are quite delicious. How is the cedar tree coming along? I do hope it grows well out there and the heat and the frosts don't kill it!

I have no more news and look forward to receiving your next letter in due course.

My fondest love to you all as always,

Emmy

Grace rolled onto her back and stared at the ceiling, the tears rolling down her cheeks as she first absorbed and then digested the contents of the letters. The two sisters obviously had a close relationship and she pondered over how Emmy must have felt when she found out about David dying. She started, sitting up abruptly. Why didn't Jane finish her letter to Emmy? Did she succumb to the flu as well and die? Maybe Emmy didn't find out about David dying for months or longer? Her mind whirled as she tried to untangle the web of questions in her head. After carefully placing the letters back in their individual page protectors, Grace slipped them into her drawer and hurried to the study. She pulled the heavy telephone directory from the shelf and dropped it on the desk before flicking it open and running her fingers down the pages until she located the number.

"Good morning, Births, Deaths, and Marriages. Susanna speaking."

"Hi, Susanna. Grace Campbell here. I wonder if you can help me find out the approximate date of a person's death in 1917?"

"I'm sure I can get someone to help you. Just give me a few details and we will see what we can do."

Grace gave Susanna Jane McLeod's name and address, explaining that they wanted to erect a plaque in memory of the original settler. She waited anxiously, the background music failing to distract her. She clenched her teeth as the music stopped and the phone gave a click.

"Would you mind if I get back to you on this one, Grace? I'll get someone to go through the archives and see what we can find. In those days, it often took a while for the government to be notified of a bush death that occurred, so I may have to look a little deeper into it. Can I have your phone number?" Grace recited the number and waited.

"Thanks very much." Susanna replied. Grace crossed her fingers and hung up.

As she peeled the vegetables for dinner, the image of Henry Dawes' kind face flashed across her mind.

"He'll be really interested to hear about all this." She smiled to herself. For the moment though, she would keep her findings to herself.

CHAPTER 21

The men were focused on greasing and preparing the machinery in readiness for harvesting. Spring had sprung and before they began in late October, they needed to get the ewes and lambs in again.

They had marked as many little newborn lambs as they could after shearing, but there could be hundreds of lambs out there now with fat little tails covered in manure from the season's fresh green grass—just waiting for the flies to lay their eggs in, causing the emerging maggots to eat into the lambs' flesh. Grace cringed at the thought of the terrible pain and possible death that often occurred. The only kind way of managing the problem in this climate was to remove the tail by fitting a rubber ring around it allowing the tail to numb, then shrivel and drop off within a few days. This method was also used to castrate the male lambs, and while they were being held for the process, they were vaccinated and had a colour-coded identity tag clipped into their ear, recording the property identification number and year of birth.

Grace and Daniel had shifted their bottle-fed lambs to the holding paddock outside the woolshed. Only needing a milk feed twice a day now, they were grazing and very keen to eat any of Grace's new plants if they could. When the flock had been brought in, Pete said they would have to join them, in spite of Daniel's protests. Grace hoped they would still come when they were called—for a while anyway, but she was still working on convincing Daniel of the benefits of this new set-up.

While the men were busy, Daniel played outside with Min and Grace dialled Georgie again. She had called Grace back following her previous attempt at contact—but Pete had been in a foul mood and had just come inside for smoko. Grace had quickly said, "Can't talk," and hung up.

They often went long periods without contact but seemed to be able to pick up exactly where they had left off. To Grace, that was confirmation of a valued and sound friendship.

She dialled, sitting in the office chair, idly swivelling as the ringing droned on.

"Hello." Georgie was breathing heavily.

"Hey, Georgie. What's doing? Sounds like I made you run."

"Hellooo—yes, I did. Oh, you know, work, work,

work. I keep saying I'll get it under control, but then I realise another month's gone and, well, no change."

"How's Marcus the magnificent?"

Georgie giggled. "You're cheeky, you know? He's great but the life of a doctor really isn't that flash." She paused reflectively. "Sometimes I think we're just ships in the night. Apparently, he doesn't do shift work, but he leaves for his hospital rounds at five in the morning and is rarely home before at least nine or ten at night. I know that's not shift work but it's bloody long hours in my book."

Grace detected a frustration in Georgie's voice she'd never heard before and waited for more, but the line was momentarily silent. "What about your work? How'ya enjoying the new team?"

Now the team leader in a newly developed program for prevention of youth suicide, Grace wasn't sure that it was the right avenue for Georgie. She had loved being a nurse manager in her previous big public hospital. Grace chewed her lip as Georgie sprung into life again and babbled on for the next few minutes about what her team were doing and how important it all was. Her enthusiasm certainly wasn't lacking anyway.

"That's great. I'm glad it's working out for you. So, when are you coming out to Whoop Whoop for a visit?"

"I promise we'll visit soon. What happens there this side of Christmas?"

"The races are held in town in November. I doubt

you'll want to be here much after that anyway unless you want to cook yourself?"

"Gets a bit hot then, does it?"

"Apparently. It's all relative, but this is western Queensland so forty to forty-five degrees most days seems to be the norm—for a couple of months anyway."

"Yikes, that's a bit hot for this little black duck. We might have to wait a bit."

"Good plan. It should be nice weather in November and hopefully not too hot. It'll be great to see you both anyway. I might ask if Beth can mind Daniel and we can stay in town so we can really enjoy the weekend. The races start at lunchtime on Saturday, but it's a huge weekend and hundreds of people come. They have a party in the evening, and then a big breakfast get-together again on the Sunday morning. That is, if you can face it."

"Oh, that sounds great. You know me—love a party and I don't mind a flutter on the horses either. Bugger."

Grace recognised the distraction in Georgie's voice. "What are you doing?"

"Painting my toenails and I just dropped the brush."

"Oh. You'd better deal with that—talk to you again soon."

"Okay, see ya."

Grace smiled as she put the receiver down. She couldn't remember the last time she had painted her toenails and studied her squarely trimmed finger nails, the in-ground dirt staining her forefingers. It seemed that even when wearing work gloves most of the time, keeping nice hands and nails was an impossibility. Grace didn't mind – she wouldn't have it any other way.

The sun was getting low in the sky as Grace and Daniel rode the quad bike to the woolshed to feed the lambs. The skies out here in western Queensland still astounded and transfixed her. Their colours, the clouds, and glorious rainbows never ceased to amaze, and this evening was no exception. As the lambs sucked ferociously at their bottles, the sky turned from apricot to deep orange, then pinks moved in as the sun slowly sank to meet the red soil and outline the black silhouettes of the gum trees.

"It's really nice living out here, isn't it? I love it."

"I do too, Mum. Beff's my best friend."

Grace smiled as she wrapped one arm around him and picked up the empty bottles with the other. "So, you like going to Beth's?"

"Yep. Beth plays games with me and we do lots of singing." He bounced excitedly as Grace helped him onto the bike. "Beff said I can call her Nanny Beff if I want to. I can't call her Nanny, cause I already have a Nanny."

Grace smiled at his logic and nodded in agreement. "We'll have to see if Nanny and Poppy will come and visit us soon. Won't we?"

A look of anxiety washed over his little face as he shook his head. "Maybe. Dad says they're too old to come."

Grace raised her eyebrows as she started the bike.

Oh really? So now, not only are our phone calls restricted, we are not allowed to have them visit either.

Her insides clenched as the mixture of sorrow and annoyance clouded her mind. Torn between her family and friends, who she loved so dearly, and her controlling husband, feelings for him slid a little further into the mire.

CHAPTER 22

That night, Tom phoned to say he would be flying up on the weekend. October was here and temperatures were rising. Some days it was already well over thirty degrees and Grace hoped she would make it through summer. She hated the heat, her fair skin frizzling under the burning Queensland sun. She had changed her routine to suit the climate and now completed her outdoor chores early in the morning and late in the evening—leaving cleaning and cooking for the heat of the day when the overhead fans provided a gentle breeze under which she could comfortably work.

After breakfast the following morning, Pete announced he and Greg were going for a drive to check the bore lines.

"Can I come too, Daddy?" Daniel was so used to his requests meeting refusal, his question was half-hearted and tentative.

"I guess so. Get your boots and hat on then."

Daniel raced delightedly to the veranda, Grace following closely as she tucked an apple and water bottle into an insulated bag for him. "Okay. I think I'll go for a ride on Jarrah. She needs the exercise, and so do I." She breathed deeply and slowly, her strength gradually returning as the need to escape became her focus. It was eight o'clock so she would have a couple of hours before the sun rose too high.

They cantered along the fence line for twenty minutes before Grace slowed the sweat-glistened Jarrah and drew a deep breath, her face flushed with heat and enjoyment. Turning down into the creek bed, she leaned forward in the saddle, frowning at fresh dingo tracks in the moist patches and making a mental note to talk to Squire.

With the cobwebs in her head blown away, Grace dismounted and dropped her reins on the ground under the tree. She patted Jarrah, trusting her to stand, swishing flies with her tail while she waited. After climbing to the top of the sandstone pinnacle, Grace sat on a flat rock, the hundreds of hectares that made up Tullagulla spreading out in front of her. In the distance, a white speck crossed the land, a trail of dust in its wake.

The ute. She was glad that Greg was with Pete; that way at least there was a chance of Daniel enjoying his morning out. It puzzled her that Pete was so disinterested in his son. Considering he hadn't received much attention from his own father, she'd really thought he would be the opposite with Daniel.

As she brushed the sweat and sticky flies from her face, she pondered idly over life and the conflicts that had occurred on this vast area of land. Jane had been walking around the homestead again. Grace was pleased she could now name her ghost instead of giving her the title of 'The Lady of Tullagulla'.

Noting these events in her diary—what was happening in the house and within her relationship with Pete when she appeared—she was beginning to piece together a disconcerting pattern. On the nights she was feeling down or anxious over friction with Pete, or when Pete was angry or abusive, Jane appeared. Did she come to talk to her? Or was she trying to warn her about something? Perhaps Jane was always there, and Grace just didn't hear her on the nights she slept well? Maybe her own relationship with Angus McLeod had been an unhappy one. She had also noted that on two occasions now, their bedroom door had slammed shut as Pete had been about to enter the room. Assuming it was due to a sudden breeze, she had thought nothing of it, but now she wondered.

With the flurry of questions rotating around in her head, Grace spoke out loud. "Is she looking for something or someone? No one else has mentioned hearing her or seeing her—only me and Daniel."

Grace felt no fear, questioning the reason why. A gentle breeze brushed hair across her face, waking her from her reverie. She would tell Tom about Jane next time he came. She was sure he would understand and believe her, unlike Pete. With the problem temporarily resolved, she stood and scrambled back to her patiently waiting horse.

Delighted to see Tom again, Grace was disappointed when he confessed he could only stay for two nights this time. He seemed distracted this visit, anxious to check on the new cattle but she was sure he had more than the cattle on his mind.

Twice Grace found herself alone with Tom, but for such brief durations there was no time to tell him about the letters. Like a cat on a hot tin roof, she dashed around completing her routine jobs automatically, her mind unable to dwell on anything except the letters. She suspected Tom was aware of her abnormal behaviour but didn't question her. Pete noticed nothing.

CHAPTER 23

*D*aniel was due for his vaccination and, of course, there were the usual food supplies to restock. So the morning following Tom's departure, Grace announced at breakfast that she was going to town for the day. She was a bundle of nerves, waiting for Pete's inquisition. He had never actually prevented her from going, however, whenever she mentioned the need for a trip to town, he seemed to insist he needed her immediate help with trivial jobs around the place—like holding timber while he sawed it or sitting in the driver's seat of a tractor and operating the levers while he fiddled with something under the bonnet. On some of these occasions, he'd delayed her so much that a trip to town was out of the question. *Is it deliberate?* She didn't know.

Surprisingly, he looked up from his breakfast, egg stuck to his bottom lip, and nodded.

"You can call into the transport company while you're there. There should be a box with some new bits and pieces for the header. We need to get it ready for harvesting next week."

Pete's need for control was more noticeable to Grace than it had been when they'd first arrived and her concerns ran deep. She had never given him a reason to not trust her and didn't seem able to get through to him that they were a team.

"No worries." She responded lightly, her heart soaring.

After hiding her mobile phone deep in her handbag, Grace loaded Daniel and a spare esky into the Land-Cruiser, switched on the car fridge to chill and drove out of Tullagulla before Pete could stop her. The folder with Jane and Emmy's letters rested securely in the back of Daniel's little backpack, hidden by his books and lunchbox.

As the silos of town drew closer, Grace was pleased with the diversion of calling into the local park. With Daniel cheerfully playing on the swings, she pulled her phone out of her pocket and rang her friend.

"Hey, Georgie. How're things going?"

"Hi there. What's new?"

Grace never could hide anything from Georgie. It was as if she had antennae, and within a few words knew when Grace needed to talk.

"Hang on a tick. I just need to shut the office door. Where are you? You sound a bit worried."

"Yeah, nothing gets past you does it?" Grace

laughed. "We're in the park in town. Daniel's having a play and I really wanted to talk."

"Okay—spit it out."

Drawing a deep breath, she launched into her spiel, "I've found some letters that date back to 1917 and I can't bring myself to talk to Pete about it cause he doesn't believe in ghosts or spirits. And anyway, I don't seem to be able to do anything right at the moment and he is always angry."

"Whoa, stop. What do you mean about ghosts and spirits, and why is Pete always angry?"

"Okay, since we have been at Tullagulla, both Daniel and I have sensed a presence a few times of a woman being there. Just in the house, and mostly outside Daniel's bedroom or in the lounge between his room and ours. I dismissed it at first and then tried to find out what women had lived at Tullagulla before, in case it really was a ghost and I needed to be concerned. But I couldn't find out anything much, except now I have these letters." She paused, unsure if Georgie was listening.

"Wow. Go on. What are the letters?" Of course she was listening.

As Grace poured out the story of the letters and the secrets they contained, she sensed Georgie's growing interest, aware of her loud intake and slow release of breath. "So, what do you think?" Grace finished.

"I'm blown away, excited, and puzzled over why Pete's not interested?"

"I don't know what's happening to Pete. I wonder if

he has always been like this but because he was away so much, and we lived so close to Mum and Dad, I never really noticed it. But here, well, he's just different."

"How different? In what way?"

"He seems angry most of the time and won't let me ring Mum and Dad or you when I want to. Says it's a business phone and I don't need to talk to other people. You know we don't have mobile reception, so I can't use my mobile, and anyway, he smashed my phone so it was out of action for a while. Now I tend to hide it!"

"Oh, my God, Grace. That's not normal behaviour. Look, we need to talk more, but I have a client waiting outside. When can I ring you?"

"That's just it—you can't or Pete will think I am going behind his back. He's become so suspicious and controlling over what I do or say now. I know I probably sound paranoid, but I am even becoming fearful talking to Beth, the other lady on Tullagulla too much, in case he gets upset."

"Right, when are these races we talked about again?"

"In three weeks. Are you still coming out for them?" Grace crossed her fingers in hope.

"Yep. Shall I ring and book a motel room or will you? I'll leave you to organise Pete. He will come, won't he?"

"Oh, yes. He is looking forward to them. I heard him asking the men the other day if they go, but Greg and Beth have been so often, they're not going to bother this year. And Squire never goes. I think Pete thinks it will be a chance for him to get together with some of the other local blokes for a good yarn and a few drinks. I asked Beth if she would have Daniel for the Saturday night so we can stay in town and she said she would love to. So I'll book the motel rooms for all of us." She fiddled with her ponytail as she spoke. She'd hoped it would be a chance for a nice social weekend for her and Pete.

"Right. You get on and do what you have to do, and ring me again when you get a chance."

Grace swiped the red icon and slipped the phone back into the bottom of her bag. "C'mon, mate. Time to go and collect the stuff for Dad now, then we'll go to the doctor and pick up the shopping."

Daniel ran towards the car, giggling as Grace pretended to race him, letting him reach the car just ahead of her.

"I win, I win." Daniel raised his fists joyfully as Grace pushed the button to unlock the doors.

The car was loaded with parts and groceries as they headed out of town and towards Tullagulla. Grace's pulse raced as she considered Henry and what he would think of the letters. She prayed he would be home, having checked in the library first and not found him there. She must remember to ask him for his phone number.

The sleepy little cottage welcomed her as she pulled up in front and opened the car door. Released from his car seat, Daniel raced confidently to the veranda, knocking as he called out, "Hello?"

This time, Henry appeared from the darkened hallway, his face beaming as he threw open the screen door and reached for Grace's hand. "You're just in time for a cuppa, or some of my rhubarb cordial?"

Grace relaxed, warmth engulfing her as she glanced at Daniel's happy little face. It was strange how content they both felt here with this lovely old man, even though they had only visited a few times.

Waiting until they were sitting at the kitchen table with a delicious pale pink rhubarb cordial drink in front of each of them, Grace reached into Daniel's backpack and pulled out the folder. "I have found something, Henry, and I want to share it with you."

His interest seemed to spike, his eyes widening as he leaned forward, pushing his glass to one side. Grace placed the plastic sleeves on the table side by side. Glancing at Daniel, she was relieved to see he was occupied with his new miniature truck—her reward for him being a brave little boy when having his injection—and she smiled as she focused on the pages in front of them.

She had carefully unfolded each page and laid them back to back in plastic sleeves, so the letters could be read without touching or damaging the fragile sheets of paper. Fumbling with his glasses, Henry peered through the lower section of the lenses as he strained over the faded ink.

"It's very hard to read. Would you like me to read

them to you?" Grace hesitated, not wanting to insult the elderly man.

"That would be great, lass. The old eyes aren't quite as good as they used to be."

Beginning with the first letter from Emmy to Jane, Grace began. She had reread the letters so many times now, she knew them by heart. As she reached the mention of the cedar tree, Daniel piped up, "We've got a cedar tree. Haven't we, Mum?"

"We have, mate. And the tree in this letter is the exact same one, only now it's very old and very big."

The concept was too much for Daniel. Losing interest, he slithered to the floor to unpack his backpack and see what it held. Henry was riveted, his head slightly turned to better hear Grace as she continued reading to him.

As she finished the final letter, Henry gazed at her. "Well, I didn't expect that."

"I know, isn't it amazing and interesting? I contacted Births, Deaths, and Marriages in Brisbane after I found these, and they were able to check records for me. They have a Jane McLeod's death listed as twenty-fifth of September 1917. I don't know the cause of death, but it seems likely from her letter to Emmy that she must have also contracted the flu and died."

"I agree. Last time we talked, you said you and Daniel had both experienced the feeling that a woman's ghost or soul roams the house. Are you thinking it is Jane?"

"Yes, who else could it be? But I don't really understand why only Daniel and I have seen her? I wonder if she is trying to tell us something, or warn me of something?"

Henry pondered, rubbing his chin. "I guess you will find out in due course? Strange that your husband has never felt her though?"

"Hmm, he doesn't exactly believe in ghosts or anything like that, and maybe Jane knows? Perhaps she's trying to be a friend or some sort of guardian for us? Do you think she's buried somewhere near the cedar tree too?"

Henry frowned. Standing, he gathered the glasses and biscuits from the table. "If she is, I would think there would be some sort of headstone there? Mind you, from what Jock told me about old Angus, he would probably have been too miserable to pay for a proper headstone. Even if he did, it's so long ago. It could be buried in dust and dirt from years of droughts and floods."

Grace glanced up at the clock, her chest tightening, aware they would be home later than Pete expected. "I have to get back to Tullagulla, Henry. Had some parts to collect for Pete and he'll be waiting."

"Of course, lass. Just hang on a minute while I pick you some fresh tomatoes."

Grace loaded Daniel and his backpack into the car as Henry appeared with a box of tomatoes, lettuce, and fresh beans. Giving the old gentleman a hug, she thanked him and slid into the driver's seat.

Her head filled with the day's events and conversations, Grace glanced in the rear-vision mirror, the sight of Daniel's sleeping face melting her heart and sending a ripple of joy through her body. She turned the volume up on the radio and settled in for the long drive home.

CHAPTER 24

*B*ack at Tullagulla, Grace worked quickly. With the car unpacked and Daniel playing quietly on the floor, she was peeling vegetables by the time Pete's ute clattered to a noisy halt outside the gate.

Preparing for the onslaught, her knees shook with relief as he threw the screen door open, smiling as he scooped Daniel up and hugged him. "How'd ya day go? Did you pick up those parts for me?"

"Good thanks. Yep, they're just sitting on the bench in the shed next to the car." She smiled, rising on her toes to meet his unexpected kiss.

"What's for dinner?"

Grace laughed at the repetition of his nightly question. "Steak and vegies with gravy, and strawberries and ice cream for dessert."

"Yummo, hey, Daniel. Our favourite."

Grace's eyes prickled as Daniel turned to his dad with an adoring look. She wished she could freeze the rare, happy moment. *What was going on to put Pete in such a good mood?*

It didn't take long to find out.

"Hey, you know the races are coming up soon in town. I thought we'd go and make a weekend of it?"

"Sounds great. When I last talked to Georgie, she mentioned they would like to come out for the race weekend as well." She kept an anxious eye on Pete's face, unsure how well her suggestion would be received.

"Great. The more the merrier. I've been talking to some of the neighbours on the two-way and it sounds like it's a great social weekend. Ring up and book us a motel, will ya? I'll just hop through the shower while dinner's cooking."

It took all Grace's strength to control her inner relief, her hands pressing heavily on the edge of the kitchen bench as she focused on breathing calmly and deeply. Never knowing how Pete would respond to every suggestion and situation still confused and frustrated her. When she expected him to object, he didn't, and when she least expected it, sometimes not even knowing what she had said wrong, he would fly off the handle and turn into a raging bull. She really had expected some resistance from him over the race weekend and sent up a silent prayer that he had mentioned it first. With harvesting about to begin, the whole anxious event tested even the most placid of farmers.

Shrugging, she shook her head and placed the

onions and pieces of steak in the pan on the wood stove. The sizzling and spitting distracted her as she stepped backwards away from the steam.

Tom arrived again as they were two weeks into the harvest. Grace was determined that on this visit, she would tell him about Jane and the letters she had found.

It was late in the afternoon, and Pete and Greg were transferring the grain from the field bin into the truck to take into the silos when Tom turned to Grace, his face almost pleading. "Have we got time to go for a quick ride? I haven't been on a horse for a few weeks now and am a bit concerned I will forget how."

"You sound like a little kid." They both laughed. "Haven't you heard that it's like learning to ride a bike, or how to swim? Once you know how, you might get a bit rusty but you don't forget. Come on, then. We'll see if Daniel can have an hour with Beth and give Spike and Jarrah a quick ride."

Once they had mounted and headed down past the woolshed, Grace halted, waiting for Spike to catch up so they could ride side by side. "I've got something to tell you."

Tom opened his eyes wide as he quipped, "Uh-oh. That sounds mysterious. Go ahead then. I'm all ears."

Grace downloaded the whole story of hers and

Daniel's experiences with the ghostly presence, and then her discovery of the letters.

Tom's joking turned to solemn wonder. "Wow. That's incredible. I can't wait to read them."

"Pete doesn't believe in ghosts so I haven't told him about them yet. He's not interested in anything historical. I've shown them to Henry though and I've told my friend Georgie. So, what should we do? Tullagulla is your property." Grace waited while Tom digested the story, staring thoughtfully at her for a full minute before he spoke.

"I would really like to take the letters back to Melbourne with me. One of my regular clients is an historian and I'd like to discuss it with him. We need to have the history and the letters recorded and archived safely, and you never know, we may even be able to find out more. I can keep copies of everything here and put together a written record of Tullagulla's history, as much as we know so far anyway. What do you think?"

"That sounds like a good place to start. So you do believe me then?"

"Oh yes, Grace. I not only believe you, but I think Jane, and Tullagulla, have been waiting for someone like you to live here in order to reveal herself."

Grace breathed a huge sigh, dizzy with relief that Tom had not only listened but he believed her and was prepared to follow it up. Documenting and securing the history for all time was a bonus.

Before he left for Melbourne again, Grace slid the

letters inside a folder and slotted them into his bag while Pete was out of the house.

As Tom said his goodbyes to them all, he gave Grace a knowing smile and the weight of responsibility tumbled from her shoulders.

After opening the fire box of the wood stove, Grace stirred up the embers, lifting her head in surprise at the sound of men's voices raised in anger.

Is that Pete and Greg arguing? She had never heard Greg raise his voice and Grace frowned, puzzled about what could have possibly caused this yelling match.

Probably Pete's fault. She shrugged her shoulders. *Nothing new. He's not afraid of yelling at anyone, and he is always right. Just a matter of time before his true colours showed through to the men, if they hadn't already, and they yelled back.*

Guilt coursed through her veins as she listened to herself, reflecting on her sarcasm. She didn't much like the person she seemed to be becoming and had taken note of new lines that had appeared around her eyes.

She threw a few small pieces of wood in to the fire box before opening the flue and filling the kettle. "I have grown to quite like you, you cranky old hunk of junk." She spoke out loud to the wood stove. "Just wish you weren't so bloody hot." She smiled at the irony. The old ceiling fan cranked overhead, stirring the air slightly, and she turned to the portable evaporative cooler, gobbling up the tank water as it blew its gentle damp breeze towards her. "And as for you, well, I suppose you're better than nothing."

The yelling stopped, and Grace tensed as the gate slammed and Pete stomped up the path. "You've been at it again, haven't you?"

Grace raised an eyebrow as her body stiffened involuntarily. "What are you talking about?"

"Planting lucerne. Little Miss Smarty Pants has been mouthing off about what a good idea it would be to plant lucerne in the grain paddocks we've just harvested. I'm the manager here, not you. If you wanted to be the manager, you should have applied for the job."

"You sound like a petulant five-year-old." Tired and fed up with Pete's ranting, Grace snapped. "I think it is a good idea and you should discuss it with Tom. He's the boss and will make the decision either way. Yes, you are the manager here, and you should be listening to everyone's opinions instead of just being a dictator. We're all part of a team, including you."

As soon as the words were out of her mouth, she realised her mistake.

Pete's arm shot out, grabbing her by the back of her neck and turning her to face him as he drew her close, his eyes deepening to a stormy grey in anger. "Don't you dare speak to me like that. Whoever you think you are, you are not as good as you think." He squeezed his fingers into her neck, forcing Grace to squirm and twist her shoulders as she reached up to push him away.

"Leave me alone!"

"Oh, I will." Sneering, he turned, slamming the kitchen door as he walked down the corridor.

Collapsing on a chair, Grace rubbed her neck gingerly, aware she would have two purple bruises by morning. Thumping the table with her fist, tears sprang from her eyes. *Bugger him. Now I will have to leave my hair loose for days to cover the bruises.* A tear ran down her cheek as, boiling with fury, Grace stomped to the bathroom to wash her face.

The suggestion of planting lucerne had been hers and it was a good one. She recalled the discussion about it with Tom just a couple of days before, when she had taken him out to the paddocks being harvested to inspect the progress.

"Good enough to plant lucerne into really." Her comment had been random, however, Tom and Greg had been intrigued and Tom, in his humble way, had pressed her for more detail.

Aware that Pete had been on the opposite side of the paddock, Grace elaborated. "Well, the subsoil moisture is pretty good now after the last rain, and lucerne is great because of its sustainability. Plus the paddock is nice and clean, so it would make a good seedbed for lucerne."

"And?" Tom had queried. Both men had had their eyes glued on her.

"Provided we jag a few good storms through the

summer growing months, it will last four or five years before the paddock would need to be re-sown. It's a highly nutritious legume and makes great cut-and-come-again feed. Plus, if we get a really dry spell, it will be the last feed to die off and the first to come back after rain. We could also put the ewes and lambs in on it during the winter if needed.

Clearly distracted, Tom had digested the information in silence. As butterflies had taken flight in Grace's stomach, she prayed silently that if the subject of lucerne came up again, the men would let Pete think it had been his idea.

Apparently not.

CHAPTER 25

*G*race removed her dress from its protective cover and hung it on the wardrobe door handle. Her insides were leapfrogging all over the place—a mixture of excitement and anxiety. The bruises on her neck had faded to pale green and yellow but were still tender to her touch. Waves of despair coursed through her body every time she brushed her hair.

She had hoped to sweep her hair into a classy chignon and pin the pretty fascinator into it, relieving her neck of the hot weight in the early summer heat. Now she resigned herself to having to leave it loose for the picnic races, and instead wear her wide-brimmed straw hat, albeit trimmed and prettied up with pieces cut out of the fascinator. She stared at the dress, hoping it would still fit her. It was a pretty jade-green silky fabric, slim-fitting with tiny capped sleeves and finishing well above her knees.

With memories of its last outing, she smiled. It had been such a happy day—her brother and sister-in-law's wedding. She had been several weeks pregnant with Daniel and was glowing with health and vitality. In the early throes of love, she had been proud to parade her gorgeous-looking husband around all her relatives.

Now the mirror on the wardrobe door reflected a thin, pale face, beads of perspiration surrounding her hairline and her petite, wiry body clothed in dirty denim jeans and a floral cotton work shirt. Its sleeves were rolled to her elbows, and both top buttons were undone to allow any cool breeze access to her clammy skin.

The weather forecast for the weekend was for warm, sunny days with a gentle breeze. She hoped they were right, at least where the breeze was concerned.

Grace lay her dress on the top of the neatly packed toiletries, underwear, and casual gear. Pete's good trousers and shirt were folded carefully, his rarely worn, one and only tie in a plastic bag tucked in the side pocket. She would give them all a freshen up with the iron at the motel. After closing the suitcase lid, she zipped it up and stood it in the corner of the room.

Right, now Daniel's stuff.

He was excited to be having a sleep over at Beth and Greg's place. Armed with Greg's promise of a fire in the backyard fire-pit to toast marshmallows, Daniel leapt around with excitement, his shrill voice an octave higher than usual, his three-year-old ears deaf to his mother's instructions. "Daniel, listen to me."

He was spinning around in circles. Grace's voice finally penetrated his excitement as he came to a dizzy halt, crashing sideways into the wall.

"Settle down, mate." Grace grasped his arm more firmly than she meant to in exasperation. "Come on. You bring your backpack of toys, and we'll go over to Beth's now."

"Ouch. You're hurting me, Mummy."

"I'm sorry, mate. Just come on now. Beth will be waiting for you." She opened the bathroom door and, raising her voice over the splashing of the shower, called out, "I'm just dropping Daniel over to Beth's. When you're ready, would you please put the suitcase in the car?"

" Okay, will do. Shit." Grace giggled at the silhouette of Pete through the frosted glass. *Obviously that thud was the soap dropping on his foot.*

Finally. What have I forgotten?

Climbing into the car, she glanced at Pete, scrubbed up and looking pretty darn good in his blue shirt and casual shorts. He was in an exuberant mood, smiling and chatting much more than normal. The knot in Grace's stomach began to relax and unravel as her anticipation of them enjoying a happy weekend together increased. She turned up the music and they both sang on and off as they drove along the dusty road towards town.

Pulling into the motel car park, Grace spotted Georgie near the gate of the motel swimming pool, her focus on a gorgeous blonde-haired goddess emerging from the water.

"Georgie. We're here." Grace leaned out of the window waving madly.

As the car came to a halt outside the motel office, she leapt out before reaching up and hugging her friend. Stepping back, they assessed each other, smiling and hugging again. Georgie turned to Pete, giving him a brief hug in turn. Suddenly aware that his attention was elsewhere, a shaft of fear shot through Grace as she followed his gaze.

Georgie reached out to the blonde woman, appearing anxious to introduce her. "This is Tara, a work colleague who has come for the weekend instead of Marcus. Unfortunately, Marcus had an emergency at the hospital and sends his apologies." She paused, doubt clouding her face before she continued, "Anyway, Tara was keen to come. She has just been through a broken relationship and wanted to get away," Georgie finished lamely.

Grace reacted first, embarrassed by Pete's fascination with Tara's breasts bursting over the top of an incredibly skimpy bikini.

She reached out to shake the young woman's hand. "Hi, nice to meet you."

Pete woke from his reverie, squeezing Tara's hand, holding it just a little too long. His ear-to-ear smile left no doubt of his welcome; he seemed unable to tear his gaze from her slim, shapely figure and beautiful face. Her skin glowed gold, still shimmering with water from the pool and her wet, blonde hair fell elegantly over her shoulders as she released it from its clasp on top of her head.

"Okay, guys. Shall we get settled in our rooms and meet over at the café for a quick coffee before we dress for the races?" Grace was anxious to break Pete's stare, shoving him slightly with her elbow.

"Yep, righto. I'll just get our bags while you check in." He nodded towards Grace, smiled at Tara again, and returned somewhat reluctantly to the car.

Grace bent to slip her sandals on, her nose twitching as she suppressed a sneeze.

"Geez, go steady with that aftershave, Pete. You'll have us all choking with asthma with the amount you're spraying around."

Pete grinned, lifting his chin as he leaned towards Grace. "Smell irresistible, do I?"

She gave him a gentle shove, smiling up at him. Her stomach had re-knotted itself in anxiety, uncertain now that them coming into town was such a good idea.

Chiding herself, she straightened her shoulders and scooped up her bag from the bed. "C'mon, Romeo. Stop looking at yourself in the mirror and lets get down to the racecourse before they finish serving lunch." Grace grabbed Pete by the hand, towing him gently as he took a last glance at himself in the motel mirror.

No sooner were they through the gates than the throng of brightly coloured dresses, hats, and fascinators overcame them. Music and the crackling of the loudspeaker eased Grace's fears as excitement bubbled. Pete turned towards someone calling out his name. Acknowledging a group of local farmers, he touched Grace's shoulder as he announced, "I'm off for a beer with the boys before the first race. I'll see you in the marquee in a little while."

Grace raised her eyebrows as she glanced at Georgie.

"Come on, my friend. Let's go and check out the horses and then we can head into the marquee." Georgie tucked her arm into Grace's as she gently pulled Tara with the other hand. "You can come with us so you don't get lost amongst all these men," she joked.

Feeling conspicuously like the country mouse in her now-too-loose dress, too-big hat, and her sensible low-heeled sandals, Grace studied her companions. Georgie and Tara could have been mistaken for models, more suited to Royal Ascot than a country race day. Georgie's smart, off-the-shoulder, slim-fitting cream dress would not be out of place at a Sydney fashion show or a society cocktail party. A tiny matching hat crowned her smooth dark hair, its half-veil slightly shading her flawless make-up and bright plum lips.

Tara wore red. Bright, fire-engine red. Grace considered briefly—and a little bit sarcastically—if she should offer her some sunscreen. There was certainly enough bare skin to warrant a whole bottle of it. She must have been poured into her strapless figure-hugging dress. Her blonde hair was swept into a classy knot at the base of her neck. And a bright red and black fascinator perched jauntily atop the perfectly brushed head, angled so the red and black feathers pointed to the sky, rather like antennae on an insect. Both Georgie and Tara wore high-heeled sandals—Tara's matching strappy red sandals were so high, Grace was unsure if she would get through the day without breaking an ankle.

Grace and Georgie stopped at each of the horses lined up in their open-fronted stalls, studying the form guide and matching each horse to its race history. Tara was clearly bored witless, having declared she held no interest in horses unless they were winning her money. Her gaze roved around the crowd, idly absorbing the scene and in particular the men. Out of the blue, she announced "I'm going to the bar for a drink. Which marquee are we meeting in?" she asked Grace.

"We have tickets for the Cattlemen's Marquee—the third one along. Our names will be on the list but you will have to give Marcus's name as that's who they are expecting."

"I'll find Pete in the bar and he can show me." Tara oozed confidence as she tottered away.

Georgie squeezed Grace's arm, winking as she

steered her closer to the stable area. "Don't worry about her—she's a big girl. I'm sorry I didn't get a chance to warn you before we got here. It really was a last-minute thing and I felt a bit sorry for her."

"That's okay, Georgie, really. I know you feel responsible for her but this is the country. She'll be fine. It's the blokes I feel sorry for." Grace laughed, relieved that she and Georgie could enjoy their day and catch up after all that had happened since their last phone conversation.

Between studying the horses from behind the barrier, Grace making notes on her form guide, and catching up with the latest gossip from home, the girls jumped in surprise when the loudspeaker boomed, announcing the horses for the first race.

Pushing their way through the crowd to the railing, Georgie steered Grace in front of her. "I'll stand behind you. I can see straight over your head and you can keep some of the dust off my outfit." She laughed, wrinkling her nose. "Not really the best choice of colour for bush races is it?"

Giggling, Grace nodded, turning to watch the horses line up in the barriers on the other side of the course.

Despite deciding to have a small flutter on every race, Grace had no knowledge of any of the horses other than what was listed in the form guide. She'd just thought it would add excitement to the day, even if she didn't win anything. Her budget was small, her enjoyment enormous. Georgie, on the other hand, liked to bet randomly and invested considerably more money than Grace on her choices.

The starter's gun fired and the horses bounced out of the barriers. As they drew closer to the spectators, Grace couldn't contain herself. Leaping up and down, fingers gripping the rail tightly, she shouted as the horses galloped towards the finish line. "C'mon, c'mon. Faster, faster." Shrouded by a cloud of dust, it was hard to see which was which in the cluster of horses as they pounded past the winning post. Grace swung around to Georgie. "I think that was my horse that came third. Did you see? Where did yours come?" The girls waited as the crowd quietened, hushed in anticipation for the official announcement of the winners.

Grace's joy was contagious—the discovery that her horse had come second, not third, boosted Georgie's disappointment after her randomly chosen horse coming next to last.

Following the announcement of results, the crowd drifted back to the bookies and the marquees, a mixture of emotions as some collected their winnings and others commiserated with friends.

The marquee was buzzing with groups of men and women standing around drinking and nibbling the delectable platters of titbits being handed by black-aproned catering students. Men of all ages, shapes, and sizes dressed in smart jeans or moleskin trousers and finely checked shirts, mostly with their sleeves rolled to the elbow, laughed and talked, clearly delighting in the social opportunity to catch up with friends.

Country and town women mixed together, dressed in their finest, a contrast of bright-coloured cotton and sleek satin fabrics. Most of the women's heads were topped with an equally bright-coloured hat or fascinator while the men wore a variety of their best felt or straw Akubra hats.

Grace and Georgie worked their way through the crowd to the drinks table before both selecting a glass of orange juice instead of the dominant sparkling wine.

"Plenty of time for the sparkling stuff next, hey, Gracie. We've got all afternoon ahead of us." Georgie laughed as she accepted a tiny savoury from the tray being offered by a fresh-faced teenager.

"Absolutely." Grace waved her winnings at Georgie before tucking them into her purse.

Laughing at Grace's excitement, Georgie steered her towards their table. Both women were obviously grateful to sit and take the weight off their feet.

"I wonder where Tara got to? I kind of feel she's my responsibility." A wave of worry crossed Georgie's face as they ate their delicious chicken and salad lunch.

Grace's vision clouded briefly as the two women stared silently at each other, painfully aware that Pete had also not yet turned up.

As if gifted with mental telepathy, Pete walked in to the marquee, his large frame hiding Tara behind him until they drew level with the table. It was obvious to Grace that his 'beer' had been more than just one. His smile stretched across his normally sullen face and he reached his hand back to grasp Tara's and sit her next to him.

Fury flooded Grace and she took a large gulp of her drink, triggering a bout of coughing. Turning away from the table, Grace covered her mouth with her napkin, gritting her teeth until she had regained her composure. She would not let this blonde bombshell ruin her weekend.

Unable to watch her husband flirting with Tara, Grace was pleased when race two was announced and Georgie grabbed her arm, almost capsizing her chair as she stood suddenly. "C'mon. It's my turn to win something this time."

Grace shot a measured look at Pete. "Are you two coming to watch the race?"

Pete glanced briefly at Tara before responding. "We'll finish lunch first, then we might have a look around, or we might just head back to the bar."

Grace nodded, boiling heat flushing her neck, and she allowed Georgie to lead her away.

Her nails bit into the railing as the horses flashed past her to the winning post. This time, Grace was barely aware of them. Consumed with rage and despair, she just wanted to go back to the motel and curl up on the bed.

"Come on, Gracie. Take no notice of them. Let's just enjoy ourselves. Pretend we are back at our local race day at home, when we were just out of uni." Georgie dug Grace in the ribs, imitating one of their school mistresses. "Shoulders back, eyes up, and proceed as you would to collect your prize."

Grace smiled, thinking how funny it had seemed when they were at school. It didn't seem very funny at all now. Not wanting to ruin Georgie's weekend either, she suggested they go to the tea and coffee tent.

It was quieter, and they collected their coffee and walked over to the small corner table away from the other groups of race-goers. At least here she wouldn't have to witness Pete lolling all over Tara as she drooled on him while they guzzled numerous bottles of wine.

"Tell me how you got on talking to Henry about those letters you found?"

Grateful to Georgie for the distraction, Grace downloaded her verbal report of their enjoyable visit, including the previously forgotten snippet about Henry's daughter having been engaged to Jock.

"Wow. Tullagulla really does have quite a colourful history doesn't it? I just wonder though, why Jane, if it is Jane, keeps coming to visit you and Daniel? Do you think she is trying to tell you something?"

"I don't know, but sometimes it's as though she is attempting to protect us. When I had that miscarriage, she visited me and I felt really calm afterwards. And I always seem to sense her around us when Pete is in a foul mood.

"Does he know about her?"

"No, he doesn't believe in ghosts. But funnily

enough, a couple of times when he's been about to come into our bedroom, the door has slammed in his face."

They both laughed uproariously.

"We thought it was the wind the first time. The second time he thought I'd slammed it, but luckily I was in bed when he opened it and even he realised I wouldn't have had time to slam the door and jump back into bed. I told him it was probably because he was bigger than Daniel and me and caused more of a breeze as he walked. He didn't believe me though, but that's his problem, not mine. Thankfully, it hasn't happened again."

They laughed again as Grace reached out and took Georgie by the hand. "You're a good friend, Georgie. Thanks for coming for the weekend. I'm sorry Marcus couldn't. But, well, maybe it's for the best."

Changing the subject once again, Georgie asked, "Do you know where Jane was buried? You said she wrote in her letter that she had buried David and then planted the cedar tree. Do you think her husband would have buried her there too?"

"I don't know because we haven't been able to find a headstone or anything to pinpoint her grave. Most of these older properties around here have their own little cemetery but Tullagulla doesn't seem to have one. I can't imagine she was buried in the town cemetery. I did ask Henry and he's quite sure she would have been buried on Tullagulla. He said he knows the cemetery very well and there is definitely no grave there marked with Jane McLeod's name on it. Angus is buried there though. I want to go and visit his grave one day but I haven't had the time yet."

Georgie rose. "C'mon then, girlfriend. We've missed a couple of races so we'd better go and see how much money we've won."

Grace laughed. "I hope we've both won heaps. It can be a nice little weekend-away fund for our next catch-up."

CHAPTER 26

*T*he girls cheered the cloud of dust at the final race before visiting the bookie again to collect Grace's generous winnings and Georgie's more meagre total.

"There you go. See, it's worth visiting the horses and studying the form guide. That horse you backed in the last race was the one trying to pull the stables down when we saw it. It's obviously exhausted itself and didn't have enough energy to race." Grace giggled as Georgie pulled a face.

"Right, let's see if we can find this recalcitrant husband of yours and the bimbo colleague of mine." Georgie twisted her mouth, grimacing as she rolled her eyes.

With the races over, the band were warming up and the crowd around the stage and bar was growing bigger and noisier. Unable to find either Pete or Tara in any of the marquees, Georgie stood on tiptoes, straining above the crowd at the bar to locate Pete. They were pretty sure they would find Tara wherever he was, and Georgie had made it known she was furious with herself for bringing her. It wasn't as though Tara was her friend, and now she'd confessed she had known she was a flirt.

Muttering, "Why did I bother with her," she turned to Grace.

"I can see Pete up at the bar talking to some other guys. It's too crowded to see if Tara is there but she's a big girl and I'm not going to worry about her. She knows where the motel is and can get a taxi back. Come on. Let's go and have that glass of wine and listen to some music for a while, then I suggest we catch a taxi back to the motel ourselves. That looked like a pizza place across the road so we could get some 'real food' later and see if there's a movie on Netflix?"

Grace nodded, her emotions see-sawing between despair and intense anger. Trailing behind Georgie's elegant and determined figure, she didn't have the heart to mention that her stomach was too churned up to handle either a drink or a pizza. Pete had made it pretty clear that today he preferred Tara's company to hers.

"Right. Get that down you and let's see if it puts a smile on your face." Georgie placed a plastic cup in front of her. Grace peered into the dark golden liquid before raising her eyebrows at Georgie.

"Don't ask, just drink."

Grace raised the cup to her mouth, grimacing as the fiery liquid burned its way down her throat. A warm glow took over her stomach, the nausea easing as she relaxed. "You're a wonderful friend, Georgie. Please, no more drinks though? I'll be okay."

"Right. Well, I'll ring for a taxi now and we'll forget about the others. Girlfriend night at the motel?"

Grace smiled wanly, hesitating as the wobbly jelly feeling in her legs dissipated. *At least the whisky has wiped away my misery for the moment.* She stood carefully as the warm glow spread throughout her limbs.

Georgie tucked her arm into Grace's and they walked side by side to the gates of the racecourse before peering into the darkness as a taxi drew up.

She woke with a start as a car door slammed outside the motel. A woman giggled.

"Shhhh."

Another giggle, quieter this time. Grace waited, her ears straining.

After sharing a pizza and watching a movie, Grace had given her friend a goodnight hug and returned to the motel room she had thought would offer so much more than it now did. She had sluiced away her sorrows under a hot shower and hopped into the big empty bed, tossing and turning before, eventually, sleep claimed her.

So much for a wonderful romantic opportunity.

The curtains were closed tightly, the room in total darkness. There was a rattle and fumbling of the key finding the lock before the door quietly opened. Her body rigid, Grace feigned sleep, her mind alert and as sharp as a tack.

Peeping through semi-closed lashes, she was surprised the early rays of daylight were already streaming through the door as Pete stealthily crept to the bathroom. As he crawled into bed beside her, Grace was overpowered by the stench of beer, rum, and … perfume?

She rolled on her side, her back to her husband, wide awake and paralysed with disbelief until his rhythmic breathing became heavier and the snoring began. Confident he wouldn't wake in a hurry, she tiptoed to the bathroom and picked his shirt up off the floor from amongst the heap of discarded clothing.

Her legs shook, the bile rising in her throat as she buried her nose into the fabric. Collapsing on the floor, shock froze any tears, her eyes wide open as realisation dawned. The shirt didn't just smell of the overpowering perfume Tara had been wearing—it also wore smears of bright red lipstick around the collar and down the front, as if having been progressively unbuttoned by kisses.

Throwing the shirt hard against the wall, Grace turned and unplugged her mobile phone from the bathroom power point and fiercely punched a message into the screen.

Grace: *Are you awake? Can we go for a walk?*

Georgie: *Yes, meet you outside in a couple of minutes.*

Quietly, Georgie reached into her suitcase, grabbing a clean T-shirt and shorts. After slipping on her sneakers, she backed out, closing the door carefully behind her and tucking her phone and the room key into her pocket.

Grace was sitting on the chair outside their room, her T-shirt on inside-out, dazed and pale. She touched her cold cheeks with burning palms.

After pulling her to her feet, Georgie steered her away from the motel and down to the path alongside the river before she spoke. "Are you thinking what I am thinking?" she asked Grace gently.

"What else am I to think?" Grace exploded. "He comes in after being out all night, stinking of HER perfume, and his shirt covered with HER lipstick. That's pretty sound evidence to me."

"I know. I'm so sorry I brought her with me. I had forgotten, but she behaved badly at our Christmas party last year too." Georgie was clearly devastated, no doubt blaming herself for the situation.

"It's not your fault. If it hadn't been her, he would have probably found someone else. I saw the look he gave her when they came to the marquee for lunch. He used to treat me that way." Grace crumpled as sobs wracked her body.

Georgie's arms wrapped around her friend as their

walk halted. Dragging a tissue from her pocket, she pushed it into Grace's hand. "I don't know what to say, Gracie. You don't deserve this and you know I've had a bad feeling about you staying with Pete. I can only imagine what you're experiencing now, but you know what—you're strong and you're a very special and clever lady. Whatever decisions you make with your life, you know I have your back."

Walking on in silence, Grace drew a deep breath and gave Georgie a washed out smile. "Thanks, Georgie. You're right. I am strong and I will face this and do what is best for Daniel and me. But first, we have to go back to the motel and get the lousy bastards out of bed."

"Should we drag them back to the breakfast party?"

"Hmm, no. Not sure that's a good idea. If you want to go, please go, but I don't think I could face anyone. I just want to go home to Tullagulla."

Georgie gave her friend a warm hug. "Good idea. I don't think I could stand being with Tara around there either. I think the best thing for us all would be for me to pour her into my car and get her home as fast as my little Beemer will carry her."

"Thanks."

The two women stepped out quickly, anger fuelling Grace as she silently mapped out the plan, thumping the footpath as she walked.

The sun was well up in the sky, its summer rays beating down on them by the time they returned to the motel café for coffee.

The caffeine had eased the shock and they stood to leave. Although Grace was never one to remain angry for long, she retained enough now to propel her into an efficient state of mind. Giving Georgie one last hug, she then opened the door and strode to the bathroom before gathering up her toiletries and bundling the heap of dirty clothes from the floor into a plastic bag. After jamming everything into the suitcase, she hauled out a clean shirt, shorts, and underwear for Pete, and tidied herself up. She turned off the air conditioning and pulled the sheet from him, throwing his clothes in his face. "Get up, lover. It's time to go home."

Pete groaned, rolling on his back and opening his eyes slowly. Grace stood over him, hands on her hips and a look of such fury on her face, he was instantly on alert.

"What's the matter with you? It's not time to go yet."

"Oh, yes it is. I'm packed and will be leaving for Tullagulla in five minutes. I will give you that long to dress and meet you in the car. If you don't make it in time, I'm going without you."

He swung his legs out of bed, reaching for his clothes as he glanced sheepishly at his wife. "Just give me a minute in the bathroom and I'll be there."

Grace spun on her heel and leaned the suitcase over as she pulled the extension handle out. Dragging it across the floor, she left the room without a word or a backward glance.

Outside, Georgie was packing her car and the two women smiled grimly at each other. No sign of Tara yet. Grace hoped she didn't appear until they were gone.

As she started the car, Pete opened the motel door, his shoes in his hand, and stumbled silently to the passenger side of the LandCruiser.

CHAPTER 27

On reflection, Grace was glad her silence had remained until they'd reached Tullagulla. She grimly accepted that had she tried to talk to Pete, she would have crumbled and they wouldn't have made it home.

"I'm going to Beth's. You can unpack the car and do whatever you like."

"Grace, it was nothing, honestly. You're my wife and I love you."

Uh-huh. So you admit it. Grace didn't trust herself to speak, and she turned away, almost sprinting to Beth's.

As the door opened, Beth seemed to instinctively know. Without a word, she wrapped her arms around Grace as she slumped into her motherly warmth.

"Come and sit down, love. I'll make us a cuppa."

"Where's Daniel?" Grace's voice was barely a whisper, her body completely devoid of even a grain of energy.

"He and Greg have gone in the ute to check the bores. They won't be home for a while yet. We weren't expecting you back for a few hours. Were the races okay?"

Grace nodded. "They were okay. Pete's behaviour wasn't though. I was glad Georgie was with me."

"What about her husband. Did he enjoy his weekend?"

"He couldn't come at the last minute. Georgie brought a work colleague with her who she felt sorry for because she had just broken up with her man."

At the bitterness in her voice, Beth looked surprised.

"You don't need to talk about it if you're not ready?" Grace guessed that she'd perhaps hinted more clearly than she'd realised.

Grace drank her tea gratefully before holding her mug out to Beth for a refill. After two mugful's and a generous piece of Beth's banana loaf, strength and reality crept its way back into Grace's mind and her body responded to the sustenance.

"Why don't you take the opportunity to go for a ride? Blow a few cobwebs away and you'll be able to sort out your mind a bit while you're out."

"That's a good idea. Thanks heaps, Beth. I'll be alright. Not sure about Pete though by the time I finish with him."

They smiled at each other, the frown lines easing a little on Beth's brow.

If Jarrah wondered what was going on with her owner, she never faulted. Responding to her rider's urgency, she galloped as fast as her legs would go across the flat stretch leading to the pinnacle and the outcrop of rocks Grace loved to climb. Her sides heaving and sweaty, the little mare pulled up, breathing heavily and obviously grateful to stop. Hooking her reins loosely over the eucalypt branch, Grace left her to swish flies and rest while she climbed to the top. The flat rock at the top made a perfect seat and lookout in all directions and Grace sank onto it, letting her tears flow.

Time drifted by, Grace peaceful now in spite of the increasing heat and relentless bush flies buzzing around her. With her hand waving idly back and forth in front of her face, she drew herself to her feet and rubbed the stiffness from her backside.

After sliding down over the rocks, Grace picked up Jarrah's reins and remounted. As they walked sedately back to the homestead, she gained strength from the knowledge that a temporary decision had been made. She would not mention the events of last night again.

She loved her life on Tullagulla and now couldn't imagine living anywhere else. If Pete was sheepish and felt guilty, well, so be it. She hoped he'd learned a lesson, even if the little voice in her head tried hard to argue that point. Daniel was happy here, and she didn't want to upset his life. She also knew Pete well enough to know he wouldn't mention the episode again.

Perhaps he didn't even remember? No, of course he would.

His hangover this morning had been obvious, a wicked smile warming her face at the memory of having to stop twice on the way home for him to be sick. *Karma.* Her muddled mind drifted on. Tom hadn't been to Tullagulla since harvesting. Perhaps he would come up for Christmas? It seemed he had no close family. Both his parents had passed away, and with no siblings it was only his aunt and uncle in country Victoria who seemed to occupy him outside of his accountancy business, and Tullagulla of course. She would ask him next time he rang and would give herself until Christmas was over before she would make any permanent decisions about hers and Daniel's future.

CHAPTER 28

*D*ecember arrived with a heatwave. Pete had been very quiet since the race weekend. He was sheepish around Grace and found a long list of jobs to do that kept him out of the homestead as much as possible. The arrangement suited Grace well, her anger having morphed to distrust and disrespect for her husband. If he expected trust and respect from her, he would have to earn it and with that decision made, her strength and resolve grew.

Grace's brother Brendan agreed to milk the cows for her parents, enabling them to come to Tullagulla for Christmas. The eldest in her family, Hamish, was way too busy with his Sydney legal practice to even consider bringing his family to Queensland for a visit.

Excited about seeing her parents again, she was secretly thankful her brothers and their families were too busy to come. Neither of them had much time for

Pete and she was sure they would suspect that all was not well.

In spite of the oppressive heat, Grace found extra energy, cleaning, cooking, wrapping presents, tidying the garden, and rushing around the lawn pushing the motor mower. She wanted to show her mum her new life and to be a daughter for a few days. Sometimes it seemed as though this corner of her vast continent was filled with just men and hard work. And even if she did enjoy it, to have her mum help her with simple tasks or just sit under the cedar tree with a cuppa would be equal to a holiday for her. Beth was lovely, a good friend, and so kind to her and Daniel, but, she reminded herself, she was not her mum, and had her own family and agenda to consider.

They would have Christmas lunch under the cedar tree. She would prepare salads, cold meat, and a huge pavlova, and she would borrow Beth's Christmas cake recipe. For dinner she would cook the turkey and roast vegetables, and for dessert they would eat the leftover pavlova—that was, if there was any—chocolate mousse, and fruit salad. Grace was determined that her first, and potentially her last, Christmas on Tullagulla would be perfect.

The harvest had yielded half a tonne to the hectare. Not the best, but given the conditions, everyone was satisfied. Graded prime hard, the wheat fetched the highest price possible, much to everyone's delight. The ewes and lambs had been let onto the stubble to clean it up and were looking strong and healthy, even though it was dry again. As the humidity increased, Grace was hopeful the summer storms weren't far away.

On the Thursday afternoon before Christmas, she and Daniel had a trip to town for last-minute Christmas necessities. As she drove back to Tullagulla, her mind spun as she mentally worked through the list of jobs to do before Christmas Day. Idly aware of a flock of galahs ahead on the bitumen filling up on spilt wheat, she eased off the accelerator and tooted the horn. She waited as, like giant hydrofoil planes, the birds rose slowly, weighted down by their full crops of grain, and drifted to the roadside out of the path of the oncoming vehicle.

The sky was darkening, stirring Grace from her reverie and reminding her of the need to get home before the storm hit. As the grid rattled under the vehicle's wheels, lightning cracked overhead lighting up the black horizon and followed closely by an ominous rumble of thunder.

She pulled up outside the house gate, then released Daniel from his car seat before transferring his little sleeping body onto the couch in the kitchen. No sign of Pete. She grabbed the washing basket from the laundry and ferried as many groceries as possible from the car fridge into the basket, dropping her shopping inside just as large spots of rain splattered on the dry, parched soil. As she picked up her bag and the giant pack of toilet paper from the back seat, the skies released their load and Grace was plunged under a deafening, torrential shower, soaking her to the skin within seconds.

In less than half an hour, the storm had passed and the sun set slowly in the west. A golden glistening reflection shone in the puddles—oranges, pinks, reds, and streaks of mauve and crimson. Grace bashed her gumboots together upside down to empty any eight-legged insects that had dared to attempt residence. Cautiously pushing her socked foot into each gumboot, she waited for the squishy feeling of unsuccessful eviction. All good. She breathed a sigh of relief and jumped off the step.

Grace reached for the rain gauge nestled on the corner fence post and plucked it from its framework before holding it up to the failing light. She gasped, raising her eyebrows. *Forty-five millimetres. Not a bad drop.*

Her smile widened with joy and relief. After tipping out the water, she re-homed the gauge and sprinted back to the house. Hooking the heels of her gumboots under the veranda edge, she released her feet from their rubbery grasp and brought them inside to prevent any potential invasion from insects.

Once she'd reefed open the top desk drawer in the study, she extracted the twenty-five-year rainfall record book she had bought when they first arrived at Tullagulla. Growing up in this land of droughts and floods, recording rainfall was in the blood—an essential and assumed task taken on by one or more residents of every property in the bush. Some farms had multiple rain gauges scattered around the fence-lines to establish an accurate record of rainfall in all corners of the land. It was common to have huge quantities of rain recorded on one area and not one drop somewhere else.

Christmas Day dawned, and Grace slithered out of bed and tiptoed to the veranda. The skies were streaked with pink as the glow of gold met the horizon. Within minutes, the sun would be up and she had lots to do. Her parents were arriving here early, having camped in their caravan beside the river last night, and she could barely contain her excitement as she buzzed through the kitchen.

Both Pete and Daniel were still fast asleep when she pulled her boots on at the kitchen door and headed down to the stables, Min trotting at her side.

Daniel's Santa stocking was filled with little gifts and treats and sitting on the hearth next to the empty fireplace. The tree, a branch from one of the Casuarina trees that had fallen in the storm, was propped up in a bucket full of rocks in the corner of the lounge. It was festooned with tinsel and lights and hung with baubles and Beth and Daniel's colourful homemade decorations. The bucket encasing the trunk of the tree was surrounded by festively decorated parcels of all shapes and sizes. Grace smiled, pressing her fingers together with joy and excitement. She loved Christmas and she loved giving.

The last few days had been so hectic she had barely had time to say hello to Jarrah, let alone go for a ride. The horses were all turned out into the house paddock now, but Jarrah would visit the stables every morning, just in case there was a morsel of food left for her. Sure enough, Grace laughed as she caught sight of the mare standing next to the stable gate. The other station horses were grazing nearby and lifted their heads in interest as Grace approached. Wrapping her arms around Jarrah's neck, she whispered in her ear and pulled her fingers through her mane, stroking her neck as she talked quietly. Jarrah nuzzled her, nodding her head up and down as if in thanks.

"Come inside, girl, and I'll give you a little treat." Grace opened the gate and let the mare in, closing it quickly behind her as the other horses realised some feed may be in the offing.

Pouring a dipper of horse pellets into the feed bin, Grace continued her conversation with Jarrah while she munched. "You animals really are the best listeners, aren't you?" She laughed.

As the last pellet was consumed, Grace threw a second dipper full over the fence onto the ground and called to the other horses, "Lolly scramble." Their lips twitched as they gently syphoned up the pellets, before Grace opened the gate and let Jarrah back out in to the paddock.

"Bye, girls and boys. Merry Christmas."

Smiling to herself, she patted her leg and Min raced to her side before they set off in a sprint back towards the house, Min leaping and barking with excitement as they ran.

Grace fed the chooks and returned to the kitchen, her worries evaporated for the moment.

Still no sign of life from the boys, so she turned the gas cooker on and filled the pan with bacon to sizzle over the flame.

"That smells good." Pete came up behind her, wrapping his arms around her and hugging her tight. Grace stiffened. He'd shown no affection towards her since the races. Why now? In fact, he had been sickeningly nice to her since 'that weekend', trying to make amends in the only ways he knew how while still giving her physical space. Her wariness hung on, and, tired and uncertain, she considered what she should be fighting for? He wasn't in a lasting relationship with Tara, but it had not been a one-off. And cleaning her car for her, bringing in the wood, and speaking pleasantly would not last, or make it acceptable.

Perhaps I should be more forgiving and these are the signs of new beginnings? She inhaled deeply as she lifted the pan and turned to serve the bacon.

Daniel's excited shouts jolted her reverie. The sun was high in the sky now, the food prepared, and the table was set for lunch.

"Tom's here. The plane's just landed. And Nanny and Poppy."

She caught a glimpse of the caravan roof over the hedge as they came around the house yard and pulled up outside. Tom hadn't been able to fly in yesterday as planned as the airstrip had still been too wet from the storm the previous night. The burning heat had rapidly assisted, bringing with it the mosquitos and more steamy conditions. Pete was halfway to collect Tom as she and Daniel ran to greet her parents.

Daniel leapt into his grandfather's arms as Grace reached out to her mum. It was all she could do to keep her tears at bay as she hugged first her mother, inhaling deeply the familiar fresh scent of her soft floral perfume, then rubbing her face laughingly against her father's bristly cheek.

The ute pulled up behind the caravan, Pete and Tom stepping out as they watched the family reunion. After shaking her dad's hand, Pete turned and kissed her mum on the cheek before introducing Tom to them both. Grace studied Pete's face, relieved he was relaxed and pleasant, but still too wary to let her guard down. Tom and her dad began chatting animatedly as Grace led them through the gate under the honeysuckle, the delicious smell of the turkey cooking wafting out to greet them.

Now, as they sat under the cedar tree, the balmy evening enveloped them all and Grace glanced around the circle of family and friends. Peace overwhelmed her, rendering her trance-like, as she sensed the slightest gentle touch on her shoulder. *Jane. You're here.* Greg and her dad were deep in conversation, their laughter and camaraderie obvious, while Pete watched and listened, chipping in with his opinions when he got a chance. Squire stood next to Pete, seemingly content to just listen.

In a companionable semicircle, Grace sat with Beth and her mother, their conversation random and varied as they watched Daniel and Tom playing in the sandpit. Grace smiled as Daniel squealed with joy. Tom was so good with him. He didn't seem to mind pretending he was a little kid again either.

Resting her gaze on Tom's clean, curly hair, she imagined what it would feel like to run her hands through it. Shocked at her thoughts, she glanced around the little group, relieved to see no one was even looking at her and couldn't read her mind. She absorbed the conversations, the men discussing the weather, machinery, and cattle, and the women's comparison of the best dried fruit to use in a Christmas cake.

Tom held her gaze, his face soft, kind, and smiling. She reeled as if a bolt of lightning had hit her, not unlike when she'd crawled under the electric fence, brushing it with her back as she went. Suddenly confused, her smile froze as her heart turned somersaults.

Leaping to her feet, Grace busied herself with clearing up, grateful that the tea-making process for everyone took time and allowed her to regain her composure and settle her nerves.

Eventually the contented group said their goodbyes and meandered back to their homes. Grace's parents insisted on bedding down in their caravan, which meant it was just Pete, Grace, Daniel, and Tom sleeping in the house.

Tom had stayed so many times before, and Grace had found the arrangement easy and relaxing. However, tonight the electricity in the air prickled and spiked her. *Is Tom as restless as I am?*

It was almost a relief when, on Boxing Day, they waved goodbye to her parents first, and then to Tom as he flew the Cessna overhead, dipping the wings in farewell. Less than half an hour later, Greg and Beth said their temporary goodbyes as they headed off to the coast for a well-deserved break with their family. In the aftermath of everyone's departure, emptiness overwhelmed Grace, so fiercely she thought she might collapse. She wanted to curl up in a ball and cry, prevented only by the arms of her son wrapped around her legs, his face as bereft as she felt.

With unprecedented timing, the phone rang. Their neighbours, Alan and Tess from Orden Downs, invited them over for a tennis afternoon. Pete was keen to go, clearly reluctant to be alone with Grace and Daniel, or to do any work.

The visit was a disaster and she did not enjoy one minute of it. Not a good tennis player at the best of times, she smiled as she missed shot after shot and retired early, misery gripping her insides as the searing sun beat down on her, escalating her nausea. Tess and Alan were lovely, hospitable, and friendly, and Grace was grateful they seemed not to notice her inability or discomfort. Instead, they lit the BBQ and handed around drinks and delicious morsels of food. Several families had been invited. The men stood around talking and laughing with drinks in their hands, and groups of women chatted and arranged food on platters. Children of various ages raced around, squealing with delight.

Why didn't she feel part of it all? What was the matter with her? She didn't understand herself anymore.

Daniel spent most of the afternoon clinging to her legs with shyness, only thawing out and wanting to play with the other children an hour before they left to return to Tullagulla. She was embarrassed when he threw a tantrum, not wanting to leave, and she struggled to get him into his car seat as he kicked and screamed.

Driving home in silence, Pete and Daniel both fell asleep, leaving Grace to focus on her thoughts and her driving. The spotlights illuminated the road ahead, providing forewarning of kangaroos leaping out in front of them. Grace had no idea how much alcohol Pete had drunk, but once again, it was a lot. Her wretchedness exhausted her, her relief overwhelming as she drove into the garage and switched off the headlights.

CHAPTER 29

*G*race woke with a headache in spite of having only had one drink the previous evening. It hung on all day, not helped by Pete's hangover and lack of cooperation. He was like a bear with a sore head again, disappearing into the machinery shed without eating breakfast.

Further adding to the atmosphere of melancholy, Daniel was devastated to discover his precious chicken, Lisa, lying dead in the pen when they fed the chooks. With no obvious injury, Daniel struggled to understand Grace's explanation that sometimes animals just die and we never know why.

His wracking sobs broke her heart. Holding him tightly, she brushed away her own tears and distracted him from his grief while they found a little box to put her in and fetched the spade to dig a grave under the cedar tree. With perspiration dripping down her forehead and her head pounding, Grace smoothed the final shovel-load of soil over the mound while Daniel plucked plumbago flowers off the hedge to spread over the fresh dirt. They stood in silence under the tree, the slim golden-haired young woman and the pale, sad little boy.

"C'mon, Daniel. We'll go for a ride. Lisa's gone to heaven now but she will love you forever." Taking her son by the hand, and with Min faithfully at their side, they dawdled towards the stables and yards, stopping frequently to inspect ant nests, pick up sticks, and assess new shoots emerging from the ground, now soft and moist after the rain.

Swatting flies and mosquitos with their tails, the horses were as lethargic as Grace who took twice as long to brush and saddle Jarrah than normal. With Daniel perched in front of her, she clicked the mare into a steady walk and headed down the track behind the woolshed and away from the homestead.

Passing the single men's quarters, they halted to call hello to Squire, digging contentedly in his little garden outside the building. He had fenced the area off with heavy chicken wire and filled it with hardy straw flowers, pink and white cosmos, and an assortment of vegetables. The colour palette lifted Grace's spirits, her mouth widening in amazement as she smiled at Squire. She hadn't ridden this way for weeks, aware of Squire's preference for privacy, and was surprised at how his garden had now transformed with the heat and rain.

"Your garden looks beautiful, Squire. Are those beans climbing up the tepees?" Tripods of fallen, spearlike eucalypt branches were firmly standing at the end of the garden, almost completely covered by vines dripping with red flowers.

"Yes, they are scarlet runner beans. Too many for me. I'll pick you some for the house."

"Thanks very much. We'd love that. Wouldn't we, Daniel?" She had one arm around her son, squeezing it gently as Squire stepped over towards them.

"Come on, little one. You can help me." He reached for Daniel before lifting him gently and winking at Grace.

Grace dismounted, hooked her reins over the post at the end of the garden, and followed them past the steps to the veranda, heading for the neat rows of vegetables. Glancing through the flyscreen door into the quarters, she caught her breath in amazement. The room directly in front of the stairs was the common room—a combination of lounge, kitchen, and a dining area, and covering the walls were shelves full of books of every size, colour, and thickness.

Noticing Grace's gaze, Squire enquired politely, as if serving her in a shop. "Do you like reading, Grace? I do. I don't have many vices these days except what's here." He gave her a crooked grin.

"Yes, I do love reading. Although I don't get as much time as I used to."

"Well, any time you like, you are welcome to come and borrow whatever takes your interest." His polished enunciation of each word still amazed Grace, his life prior to coming to Tullagulla remaining a mystery. And even after the months of the peaceful companionship he had offered her as they'd ridden around the property, she was no closer to finding out one iota of his past.

Squire passed her the bag of beans and Grace tied it to the D-ring on her saddle and remounted. He lifted Daniel and lowered him behind the pommel in front of her, and they waved goodbye before continuing on their quiet wander around the huge house paddock.

After returning to the yards, Grace unsaddled and released Jarrah back into the paddock with her mates.

Tullagulla was silent. With no breeze, the windmill stood still and forlorn, the windsock on the airstrip hanging like a wet rag on the washing line. Heat haze rose as the sun hovered overhead, its blistering rays beating down on the previously moist ground, drying its dark topsoil to a crust.

With lethargy overwhelming her, Grace pulled out a children's DVD from the shelf and pushed it into the player. She flopped on the couch, Daniel snuggling up next to her as his attention was consumed by the movie, allowing Grace to doze. Her thoughts drifted between the joys of living in this harsh but beautiful country, and her dysfunctional, distressing marriage.

The screen door slammed in the distance, waking Grace with a jolt. The movie had finished and Daniel was on the floor, building a structure of some kind with his Lego.

"What's for dinner?" Pete's question was barely more than a grunt.

She stared at him, silently questioning herself once more. *How did I find him so attractive to begin with? How could I not have realised that his charm and handsome ruggedness were a cover up for such an angry and abusive person?*

With as much care and good manners as she could muster, she responded, "There are so many leftovers, I thought we would have a clean-up of bits and pieces for dinner."

"Oh." He nodded as he pulled his shirt over his head and headed for the bathroom.

Later, Grace bathed Daniel, washed and dried the dishes, and returned to the lounge where Pete was watching television and Daniel continued to build with his Lego.

"C'mon, Daniel. Bedtime. We'll read some stories and let Dad watch his program."

Daniel glanced at his father. "Ni-night, Daddy." He reached out to hug his dad, his face crumbling as Pete shoved him away, unbalancing him and causing him to fall backwards.

"Go to bed," he bellowed.

Grace sprang to Daniel, picking him up as her fury rose. Turning to Pete, she hissed between still, half-closed lips. "How dare you. He is your son and only a little boy, and all he was doing was saying goodnight to his dad."

Pete ignored her, pointing the remote at the television and increasing the volume.

With Daniel now sobbing on her shoulder, she hugged him tightly. "It's okay, darling. Come on. Mummy will hop into bed with you and we'll read some stories."

An hour later, Grace extricated herself from the tangled arms and sheet around them, tucked Daniel's rabbit into the crook of his arm, and tiptoed out to the bathroom.

Surprised to see Pete come from their bedroom dressed in his work clothes, she blurted, "Where are you going at this time of night?"

"It's none of your business but if you really have to know, I'm going to fix that leak in the mobile fuel tank. Greg was supposed to weld it before he went on holidays but I noticed today that the lazy bastard ignored me. Again."

"Oh, okay. I'm going to bed. See you in the morning."

Without a backward glance, Pete strode down the corridor, oblivious to his wife, her wretchedness and despair having replaced her earlier fury.

Jane was watching.

After entering the machinery shed, Pete unscrewed the cap off the mobile fuel tank trailer, cursing loudly as the small quantity of diesel in the bottom of the tank shimmered. Reaching for an old empty drum, he shoved it under the drainage point and removed the plug. The last couple of litres of diesel flowed freely into the drum while he watched, anger raging in his head.

Satisfied the tank was now empty, he screwed the plug back into place and grabbed the drum by its handle before lifting it and plonking it on the ancient and dusty table leaning on the side wall. Perhaps if he had not been so angry and preoccupied, he would have noticed the old fertiliser bags stacked under the table, covered with thick dust. Most were empty but one was not, still a third full of ammonium nitrate. Perhaps if he had been a little more observant, he would have also noticed that the old drum into which he had drained the diesel had begun to rust out around the edges of the base. However, Pete was neither calm nor observant, turning immediately to the welder before flicking the power on and dropping the face mask down over his face.

As the sparks began to fly, in the fuel drum, pin-hole-sized fractures of rust progressively gave way under the weight of the fuel, allowing the drum to empty drip by drip. Then, increasing to a constant dribble, the diesel ran through the old timber slats of the table, and onto the bags underneath.

CHAPTER 30

*G*race placed her toothbrush back in the cup and peered into the mirror, too miserable to register that the pale, devastated face that looked back at her was actually her.

It was hot. Too hot even for the sheet, and she stretched out on her side, covered only by her thin singlet top and light cotton pyjama shorts, the fan overhead beating a gentle whooshing rhythm as it generated a breeze.

Woken suddenly, Grace sat up, fuzzy and confused. She glanced to her right; Pete's side of the bed was still flat and empty.

Was that thunder? There was no suggestion of a storm when I came to bed.

She swung her feet to the ground, stood up and wandered out to the side veranda. It was very light in spite of the absence of a moon. Puzzled by the unusual noise, she tiptoed across to Daniel's room. He was fast asleep, his head on the pillow with his bunny snuggled under his arm, and she smiled, closed the door again gently, and headed down the corridor.

As she reached the kitchen, her confusion turned to shock. On the other side of the honeysuckle hedge, a huge plume of orange flames reached high into the sky, black smoke billowing above them as explosions bombed the machinery shed, throwing pieces of steel and timber into the yard.

Mesmerised, Grace's feet remained glued to the kitchen floor for what seemed like ages before her horror spurred her into action. She ran into the office and grabbed the two-way radio as she pressed the button. "Help, help. Anyone who can hear me. Please help. Fire at Tullagulla." She threw the hand-piece down, the noise of a quad bike drawing close over the crackling and banging of the fire. She pulled on her boots then ran, jumping down the steps, out into the yard, past the garage and across towards the fire, her arms raised in front of her face as the heat hit her.

Squire rode up alongside her, yelling above the din. "Grace, no. It's too hot. Don't go any closer. It's too late for the shed. We need to save the cottage.

"Pete. Pete was in the shed working on the fuel tank." Grace's hands covered her face as further realisation sank in.

"Oh no!" Squire's normally calm face contorted in horror.

"Quick, get on." He grabbed Grace with a strong wiry arm, swinging her up behind him as he accelerated the bike in a wide arc heading past the blazing shed and over to Greg and Beth's cottage.

The heat scorched her skin, her nostrils flaring and throat choking as the fiery fingers reached out to Grace and Squire. She was barely aware of Squire's nondescript pyjamas, his lily-white legs bare, his feet sock-less, as were Grace's, their work boots meeting skinny, bare ankles.

As Squire shouted orders to Grace, he hauled the hose from its reel behind the house and connected it to the tank. On autopilot, she grasped the front hose and followed Squire's orders to wet the fence and ground on the shed side of the dwelling while he raised the pathetic stream of tank water up onto the cottage roof.

With a scorching face and clothes, Grace doused herself with the water, saturating her head and body. Her mind cleared momentarily and she dropped the hose, running back to Squire and shouting over the din of the fire, "We need to try to get Pete out."

"We can't. We can't get near the shed, Grace. It's too late." As he shouted at her receding figure, the roof of the shed caved in with a deafening crash and an explosion of sparks flew high into the sky, halting Grace in her tracks.

Oh Pete. Where are you? How did this happen?

"Help me, Grace. We need to keep hosing here." The desperation in Squire's voice resonated finally and she turned to him. He had a wet sack over one shoulder and he handed it to her as he picked up a second one, dripping wet, and thumped it on the ground while red-hot pieces of timber and metal dropped around them. Moving like a robot, Grace focused on him, following his lead and instructions.

To her, the fire seemed to burn forever. The machinery shed was a tinderbox, its hundred-year-old timbers dry and brittle. The storm a few days ago had been the only blessing, having allowed enough dampness to remain in the soil to aid the two of them in their desperate efforts to stop the fire from spreading to the cottage. As the stench of smoke filled the air and the flames died away to hot coals, two four-wheel drive vehicles roared across the huge yard—neighbours from Orden Downs who had heard Grace's call on the two-way.

Grace stood frozen with shock as her neighbours ran towards them, their voices raised above the din. In a stupor, she staggered across the yard towards the homestead, her face and arms black with soot, almost reaching the singed honeysuckle hedge before her legs buckled and she collapsed on the ground.

When she woke, vague memories hovered of someone carrying her onto the veranda and laying her on the floor before her face was wiped with a cool wet facecloth and a water bottle placed on her burnt lips.

Struggling to sit now, she cast her eyes around. She was alone.

Daniel! Her little boy. Grace rolled onto all fours before standing herself up tentatively. Chills coursed through her, her body shaking uncontrollably as she stared at the gaping hole in the yard where the old machinery shed had stood. Its structure was now a collapsed black, smouldering mess on the ground, her husband somewhere amongst it. Men's voices shouted, their blackened silhouettes moving around in front of the orange glow of embers.

Choking back a sob, she pushed through the kitchen and down the corridor to Daniel's room. She almost fainted again with relief. Overwhelming love brought a flood of tears to her eyes as she gazed down on her son, still fast asleep with his arm around his rabbit, exactly as he had been when she'd last looked. Reaching out to pick him up, she withdrew suddenly as she realised the dirty arms and hands, black with soot, were hers.

Better not wake him. It will be traumatic enough when he wakes in the morning.

As she backed away, the familiar sound of a skirt swishing along the timber floor, accompanied by a faint scent of lavender, wafted past. *Jane.*

"Oh thank you, Jane. I should have known you would be here for my little boy. Thank you. You are my friend," Grace whispered.

"Grace, are you there?" Squire's cultured tones, raised several decibels higher than usual, speared her attention.

She pulled Daniel's door towards her and walked back to the kitchen, her mind a little easier.

Squire and the neighbour, Alan, were pouring glasses of water for everyone as they discussed the events.

Turning to Grace, Alan asked, "Do you know what Pete was doing in the shed?"

"He said he was going to fix the mobile fuel tank." She caught the knowing look exchanged by the two men as her disbelief resurfaced. "Would that have been what caused the fire? The explosion?" She clamped her hand over her mouth.

"We'll know in due course. Squire has phoned the fire brigade, police, and Tom. Probably too late for the fire brigade now the fire is almost out, but they are all on their way."

Grace collapsed onto the chair as the shock took hold of her and tears poured down her cheeks. She wished her mum or Beth were still here. Surrounded by men, she had never felt so alone and in need of another woman as she became aware of her tatty, scorched singlet and pyjama shorts.

"Don't worry yourself, love. Go and have a shower and get some clean clothes on now. It will be a long night." Squire's kindness brought a fresh flood of tears as Grace stood shakily, nodding as she left the room.

The sun rose over the eastern horizon. Its pink and mauve glow turned to orange, bringing light into the room where Grace lay with Daniel. At his stirring, she struggled to open her swollen eyes, her hot and tender skin burning. Her eyebrows were fuzzy when she touched her face and she rolled out of bed.

The bathroom mirror reflected red skin with singed eyebrows and swollen eyes and lips. The memories of the night were blurred, coming back to her bit by bit as she slowly dressed and brushed her hair before tying it back from her puffy face. She was numb, disbelief freezing her into a shadow of her normal self.

Daniel wandered into the bathroom, still half asleep as he faced the toilet. He finished and climbed onto the little stool in front of the basin to wash his hands. Turning to Grace, he looked up, his smile immediately changing to a fearful frown. "What did you do to your face, Mummy?"

"It's alright, mate. There was a bad fire here last night and I got too close to it."

Daniel ran into the lounge, peering into the firebox with a puzzled look. "There's no fire."

"Not inside, love. It was the machinery shed. It caught on fire and burned down. Let's get you dressed then we can go and have a look."

Holding Daniel's hand, Grace stood silently in the middle of the yard, staring towards the black pile of smoking tin and timber, her mind and body too frozen to comprehend what they were staring at. As if on cue, the police four-wheel drive vehicle pulled up around the side of the house, closely followed by a white SUV.

Squire was still there, his singlet and pyjama shorts blackened, and his sock-less, booted feet now blending in with his legs, darkened with soot. His hair had broken loose from its ponytail—his grey beard and nut brown face covered with ash and soot. Grace acknowledged with a jolt that he had been here all night. *Poor man*. He looked exhausted. She was exhausted.

Two uniformed officers stepped down from the four-wheel drive as a woman and man dressed in plain clothes climbed out of the car.

Grace stood rooted to the spot as the woman made her way over to her. Holding out her hand, she took Grace's gently. "Hello. You must be Grace. My name's Maria and I'm a forensic officer. I'm terribly sorry to hear about the tragedy here last night."

Before Grace had time to respond, Daniel piped up. "Where's Daddy, Mum? Is he still asleep?"

Grace stared at Maria before covering her face with her hands as the horror returned.

Maria squatted in front of Daniel. "Hello, little man. Why don't you take me into the house and show me your favourite truck? I bet you have lots of trucks."

Grateful for the distraction, Grace followed Maria slowly back to the house as she desperately tried to collect her wits, Daniel's hand still tightly clutched in hers.

By the time they reached the kitchen, she had regained enough composure to know she would have to tell him the truth. He was nearly four and needed to know his dad would not be coming back.

Maria lit the gas ring and filled the kettle. Grace sat Daniel on the couch by the window, turning to face him. "Daddy isn't asleep. Daddy has died."

Daniel's eyes didn't leave her face as he thought for a minute, confusion clouding his bright blue eyes. "Do you mean like when Lisa died? Will we bury Daddy next to Lisa?" His innocence broke Grace's heart, even as his honesty and straightforwardness lightened it.

Kids are so amazing. They just say it how it is.

"A little bit like Lisa did. But because he is a person, and not a chicken, we have to do things a little bit differently. Special people will put his body in a place especially for people, not animals."

"Oh. So, will he go to heaven then, like Lisa?"

"Yes, mate." Grace studied Maria as guilt flooded through her, unable to admit to herself what hers and Pete's relationship had become. Was this all her fault?

She reached for mugs, a teapot, and the tea canister, and poured Daniel a glass of water. Blind habit forced her to follow normal morning procedure, the routine somehow soothing as Maria's quiet steady tones interacted with the subdued but high-pitched voice of her son.

Lifting her head, she numbly observed Squire bring the police to the kitchen door, waiting while they removed their boots and hats before sitting down at the table.

As the morning drifted on, so did the shock. Initially aware of the increasing number of people entering the kitchen, Grace faded into the security of the kitchen couch, voices and questions of those around her only vaguely registering in her brain, as if she was on a cliff staring down at a world she wasn't a part of.

Although framed as delicately as possible, the police

questions about the events occurring the previous night further added to her confusion and anxiety about her marriage.

It was mid-morning when she registered the familiar buzz of the Cessna. The ute rattled past the house, the volume enough to galvanise her return to the stove. She mechanically repeated the tea-making process.

Without a word, Tom strode across the kitchen, his arms stretched wide to encompass Grace's frail body. Daniel was delighted to see him again so soon, running over to him and hugging his legs.

"Hello, young man. Here, let me give you a proper cuddle." He reached out and picked Daniel up with one arm, his other remaining tightly around Grace's waist, holding her upright as her own two legs threatened to collapse once again.

"I'm so sorry, Tom." Grace's voice was barely a whisper.

"Shhh. Don't worry about anything. It was an acci-dent. We'll get it all sorted out with the help of these good people. They'll be doing a full investigation so we will be able to discover how it all happened and prevent this sort of thing from occurring again. Your mum and dad are on their way to get you."

"Are you sending us away?" Grace almost crumpled again as silent tears rolled down her pale, shocked face.

"No, no. They'll stay here for a few days while we work out what needs to be done, and then you and Daniel can go back home with them for as long as you need to recover. It's been a big shock and you need to be surrounded with people you love and who love you, not to mention getting some medical help for your poor face and hands."

Grace raised her face to study Tom's, her head spinning as an aura of light faded into the distance across her diminishing vision. As her legs buckled underneath her, her last memory was his kind, familiar face—hazel eyes dark with concern and the lines around his eyes more deeply etched.

CHAPTER 31

*R*ays of sunlight shone through the French doors from the veranda and onto the rug next to Grace's bed as she struggled to sit up. Confused, her memories flooded back as the dizziness settled and she touched her swollen and blistered lips. She choked back a sob and her gaze swung to Pete's side of the bed and his dirty work clothes in a heap on the floor beyond. Covering her face with both hands, she stilled her breath as the questions raged around and around in her brain.

"Was it my fault? Did he really go to the shed to avoid being with me? Am I responsible for his death?" Her whispers collapsed into involuntary shudders and the tears flowed down her face. She allowed herself to sob uncontrollably for several minutes before the tears seemed to run out and her focus reverted to the room. Someone was there. "Jane?"

The gentle breeze brushed her burned face as the

hint of lavender calmed her jangled nerves. Strengthened in the comfort of Jane's presence, she rolled gently off the bed and stood for a minute as the breeze faded and a sense of peace washed over her. After straightening her shirt, Grace smoothed the creases from her shorts and walked across to the bathroom. The clock on the lounge wall read ten minutes to three.

Mid-afternoon. I've been asleep for hours.

She gently patted her burned face with a wet cloth and brushed her hair. Taking a deep breath, and with new-found fortitude, she headed down the corridor to the kitchen before hesitating momentarily as she faced the onslaught of friends, family, and investigators.

Her parents had arrived, blessedly accompanied by Georgie.

With Georgie and her mother at her side, Grace barely registered the sea of faces as she answered questions and signed her statement for the police. She stared across the table at Squire, noting that although he had showered and was wearing clean clothes, his face was grey. Her heart went out to him. Without him, she would have been lost—unable to function and possibly even dead herself.

Recollections of her running towards the shed as the roof fell in came flashing back. Had she really thought she could save Pete? Pushing her chair back, she walked around the table and hugged the thin gentle man. He silently hugged her back, absorbing her unspoken message. When the police had finished questioning her,

Georgie took Grace by the hand and led her outside. They wandered over to the cedar tree and slumped down on the section of kikuyu lawn scrambling towards the trunk of the beautiful shady tree in the mid-summer heat.

"It was not your fault, Gracie. You are not, and never were, responsible for Pete's behaviour. You need to understand that."

Grace studied Georgie's face as her friend counselled her for the next hour while Grace scratched idly in the earth with a stick. As the load of responsibility began to ease from her shoulders, Grace peered at the hole she had subconsciously dug, her stick scraping on a rock. As the dirt around the edge of the rock dried, Grace's eyes opened as wide as her puffy lids would allow and she stared at Georgie.

"What's wrong? What is it?"

"This rock. It seems to have something engraved on it?" Grace worked frantically at the top of it, clearing the dirt from a small area with her fingernails as realisation crept through her veins.

"I think I know what this is, Georgie. It's a headstone." Grace blinked as her eyes became luminous pools. "I'm going to get Tom. It might be Jane's or David's?" She pushed herself to her feet and ran towards the house, throwing the screen door open as she called out, the distraction softening her grief.

Maria and the other police officer focused in surprise as Grace gasped at Tom. "Come quickly. I think we have found a headstone."

Tom instantly leapt to his feet as everyone else stared at Grace and each other in confusion.

With Tom, Squire, and her parents hot on her heels, Grace and Georgie returned to the cedar tree and knelt by the rock.

"Careful, Grace. We don't want to damage it." Tom squatted next to Grace and delicately brushed the drying earth aside. Grace's dad half ran to the car shed and returned with a small gardening fork and trowel, not before stopping at the laundry to collect a scrubbing brush, dustpan, and brush.

Within minutes, the flat piece of ancient sandstone was extracted from the soil, dusted carefully and laid on an old towel. It was only about 60 centimetres by 30 centimetres, and once washed carefully, revealed four rows of engraving. Some of the letters were too worn to read, but with the increasing group of attendees all chipping in with their opinions, the more easily recognisable characters and numbers were established. Tom wrote the inscription on a piece of photocopy paper with a black felt pen.

Jane Louise McLeod
2 March 1886 – 25 September 1917
David Angus McLeod
7 July 1914 – 22 September 1917

Grace and her parents stared at each other in turn. Martin was the first to speak. "Are we sure that Jane's birthdate is the second of March 1886?"

"It's pretty clear to me," Tom responded. "Why? Is there a problem?"

Grace turned to Tom as realisation washed over Georgie's face and she smiled, lifting her head as she spoke incredulously. "Grace's birthday is the second of March and we were both born in 1986. So, Grace was born exactly one hundred years after Jane."

"What's happening? Why's everyone looking funny?" Daniel piped up as he held his grandmother's hand.

The stunned silence exploded into a mixture of babble, laughter, and incredulous exclamations as they all drew closer to the headstone.

As Tom gave the interested visitors a brief explanation, they nodded and returned to their respective jobs, leaving all except Grace and Georgie still sitting under the tree. Georgie clasped Grace's hand and squeezed it gently, whispering, "You stay and talk to Jane. I'll go back inside and help your mum get a meal sorted out for this crowd."

EPILOGUE

*G*race studied the small group standing under the cedar tree, her heart melting with love and appreciation. It had been two months since the fire, and all those who truly loved her and Daniel were here. Her parents, Tom, her brothers and both sisters-in-law, Squire, Greg and Beth, Georgie, and her special new friend, Henry.

The days following the fire had passed in a blur before the weeks had drifted out of the fog and into more clarity. She only vaguely recollected Pete's funeral and the discussions about Jane and David's headstone before she and Daniel returned with her parents to the lush green farm on the Clarence River, allowing her and Daniel time to adjust to life without Pete.

Tom and Squire had assured her that they would care for Jarrah and the other horses and dogs, but of course Min went with Grace and Daniel as part of the family. It seemed that a few weeks of peace and familiarity was all that was needed before the hankering to return to Tullagulla became Grace's main focus. As her face and hands had healed, so had her mind, and she'd almost cried with relief when Tom phoned, inviting her to return to the station.

Now as she gazed around her, she knew her heart and mind were truly returning to something resembling their former state of being.

She had barely recognised Tullagulla. The summer storms had converted the paddocks to green. The yard where the old machinery shed had been was now a clean slate, allowing a clear view of Greg and Beth's cottage and the paddocks beyond. Inside the homestead, Grace had frozen with delight as she'd stepped into a brand-new kitchen—its clean white colonial-style cupboards a contrast to the stainless steel dishwasher, fridge, and beautiful big stove, its five-ring gas cooktop sparkling as it waited for use.

Henry had arrived at Tullagulla with Georgie, sitting alongside her in the passenger seat, his shrunken frame visible only by his battered old hat. He'd smiled at Grace and with a knowing smile, beckoned for her to join him at the back of the silver Beemer.

The boot had been filled with three beautiful potted roses.

Grace knelt now, her gardening gloves covered with wet dirt from planting as she reached out to help Henry spread mulch around. He and Squire had dug over and prepared a little garden close to the cedar tree, facing east. Jane and David's beautifully cleaned and restored headstone had been set up on a concrete stand at the base of the tree.

Henry raised his shaky voice as he spoke. "These roses are for those who lost their lives here on Tullagulla. This one is called Mother's Love and it's for Jane." Grace bent over it to admire its delicate pale pink blooms and inhale the distinctive perfume.

"This one is called David's Star, especially for little David, and this one is called Peace, for Pete. These roses will make Tullagulla a better place now for everyone." The creamy bloom of David's Star perfectly complemented the big, fragrant flowers of the Peace rose, its blooms darker cream with pink edges. Grace couldn't have thought of a token more perfect.

Even the men shed a tear. Henry's thoughtfulness and practical acknowledgement of the tragedies of Tullagulla affected them all.

Tom spoke first. "While we are all here, I'd like to say something."

Grace's stomach clenched suddenly in anxiety, the blood draining from her face as she waited. Was Tom was going to thank her for being here and farewell her and Daniel?

"I have discussed this with Greg and Squire, and we've unanimously decided that Tullagulla would not be the same without you, Grace. Not just your knowledge of farming, stock, and agribusiness, but your presence and devotion to this land. We all want you and

Daniel to stay on. Not as manager, because we don't believe we need one. What we have here now is a great team. I plan on spending a lot more time on Tullagulla and we'll all work together. What do you think? Will you stay?"

It took her several seconds to register his words as first her mother and then Georgie rushed to hug her.

With eyes prickling with tears of joy, she nodded slowly, her grin widening while everyone clapped and cheered. As the warmth spread throughout her body, she breathed deeply, strength and love flowing through her veins.

I'm home. For as long as I want to be, I'm home.

ALSO BY HEATHER REYBURN

TULLAGULLA SERIES

The Cedar Tree

The English Oak

The Pepperina Grove

A Tullagulla Christmas

FANTAIL RIDGE SERIES

Peninsula Promises

The Lupin Fields

The Scent of Promise

FEATHERWOOD FALLS SERIES

A Stranger in Featherwood Falls

Secrets in Featherwood Falls

Sparks Fly in Featherwood Falls

Clouds over Featherwood Falls

Coming Home to Featherwood Falls

A Festive Featherwood Falls

OUTBACK SKYE

Letters in Blue
Dust on the Heather
The Crofter's Song

THE ENGLISH OAK - CHAPTER 1

*S*himmering heat haze, reminiscent of an inland sea, mesmerised her. Muttering obscenities, Bronte Miller slammed her foot on the brake, thrust the gear stick into reverse and shot backwards. She paused to read the battered signpost on the left-hand side of the road. It indicated she needed to turn right.

"That's confusing," she said and squeezed the accelerator. The old car jerked forward, making the turn as wisps of steam rose from beneath the bonnet.

"Oh no!" She stared at the temperature gauge, gasping at the arrow hovering on red. Steering the car to the side of the road, she switched off the ignition and slumped over the steering wheel. As the engine stilled, a loud hiss sounded.

"Why do these things always happen to me?" Furiously, she reached under the dash, fumbling until her fingers found the lever. The bonnet unlatched with a sharp tug and Bronte threw open the driver's door, stepped onto the gravel road, and reeled as the furnace-hot air hit her. She strode to the front of the car, angrily kicking the tyre.

"I should've asked that shifty salesman more damn questions when I bought you, you heap of junk."

Perspiration trickled down her face and back, evaporating as the sun scorched her pale Yorkshire skin. Her fingers probed for the release catch and she yelped. Snatching her hand away from the hot metal, she wrapped it in the bottom of her T-shirt and tried again. This time, the spring-loaded bonnet flew up, catching her painfully under the chin.

"Ouch." Tears stung her eyes and she rubbed her face, overcome with weariness and despair. As steam and boiling water sprayed from a hole in what appeared to be a thick black hose, she jumped backwards, away from the gizzards of the old Holden.

"Mum, Mum!" a small voice cried out over the hiss of the escaping coolant.

"I'm coming Maddy." Bronte ignored the spewing steam and wrenched open the back door, released the seatbelt and lifted her daughter into the fresh air. In the few minutes since turning off the engine, the air conditioning had also stilled, and the temperature inside the old vehicle had rocketed. Maddy's face was beetroot red, her eyes distressed. Guilt gripped Bronte. Placing her gently in the shade of the car, she grasped the water bottle from the seat.

"Here lovey, drink this." The child drank thirstily.

Bronte splashed water onto her hand and wiped it across their faces, before swallowing the remnants from the bottle. After recovering their sun hats from the back seat, she plonked them on their heads and squatted next to the little girl.

The paddocks spread out in front of her, dotted with clumps of gum trees and unfamiliar scrubby bushes, and Bronte was gripped by a wave of despair.

Why did we come to this godforsaken place again? Oh yeah, that's right. A new beginning? Huh, what was I thinking?

A ridge of grey and orange rock scarred the low hills in the distance and the strip of dirt road stretched into infinity on her left. As it had been almost every day since they had disembarked from the gruelling flight from London, the sky was blue and never ending.

Turning to her daughter, Bronte swallowed hard. Her innards ached with love for her little girl. Maddy's curly dark hair formed a halo around her chubby face and a pair of bright eyes, glazed with tears, peered from under the big straw hat. She grizzled and raised a dirty thumb to her mouth, sucking briefly before plucking it out again, staring at it and screwing up her face.

"Yuck! It's dirty." Maddy said.

Bronte grunted and straightened her shoulders.

Now she was nearly five, Maddy only ever sucked her thumb if she was really tired or anxious about something. This was clearly one of those times.

Right, now what do I do? Bronte desperately tried to

recollect the salesman's advice, her excitement at the time of purchase having overridden her concentration on the detail.

"If it ever breaks down out in the bush, always stay with the vehicle, no matter what," he'd said. But what next?

She rummaged in her bag for her mobile phone. As she held it up in the air and pointed it in every direction, frustration boiled inside her. Still no signal. *So much for modern technology.*

Bronte opened the car's doors and windows and slid down to sit beside her daughter in the shade of the open door.

"Someone will come along soon. We'll just sit and wait." Muttering more quietly, she continued, "This new job had better be worth it." Her thoughts flipped back to the last time she had waited on the side of the road for help. She had been with her mother. The cold, driving rain of the Yorkshire Moors was a dim universe away.

"I'm hungry," Maddy whimpered.

Bronte searched in the foil-lined shopping bag on the back-seat floor. It had been ages since they'd stopped for lunch at the café in Goondiwindi, Gundy or whatever it was they called that town.

"Apple or muesli bar, lovey?"

"Both."

"Manners?"

"Please, Mum."

"Good girl." Bronte pulled the towel from the back

seat and spread it on the dirt. They sat quietly, while Maddy munched her snacks. Bronte's own stomach was too churned up to face food.

Sitting in a semi-trance, she shifted occasionally to stay in the limited shade of the early afternoon sun, and checked her watch constantly. Maddy had fallen asleep, her hot, sticky body against hers.

Remember what he said – stay with the car.

Torn, a little voice in her head suggested she take Maddy by the hand and walk back to the main highway. How far was it though? Sixty kilometres? A hundred? Maybe they could flag a vehicle down. *How long was it since they'd turned off the highway? An hour?* Her mind was beginning to play tricks and she chided herself. "Don't be ridiculous. We'll be fine."

She dozed in the scorching heat, while visions of home wove through her mind like a snake seeking refuge. Memories of damp and cold swirled together with the peace and serenity of the Yorkshire Moors in all their isolation and shades of mauve and green. She choked back a sob as consciousness returned and her dreams faded. The only view here was of the relentless hot sun and a glistening haze hanging over a parched landscape.

"This sure isn't Yorkshire," she whispered. Bronte's mind replayed the final conversation she'd had with her mother.

They'd left Yorkshire on a bleak, sleeting day. Jet-lagged, lonely and frayed by nerves, Bronte struggled to excite either herself or Maddy as she dragged her around the sights of Brisbane.

Bronte smiled as she remembered the joy and amazement transforming her daughter's face.

"Mum. Look. The kangaroo's eating out of my hand."

Their visit to Lone Pine Sanctuary had been the highlight of those first few days.

"You'll be right with this one," the salesman had said at the car yard. "Parts are easy to get if anything goes wrong, and there's no fancy stuff costing you extra money."

Well, he was right to begin with. There certainly wasn't any fancy stuff, except perhaps the air-conditioning—and that was more of a necessity than a luxury. Consumed with doubt, Bronte took another look around the sunburnt scene in front of her and her sleeping daughter snuggled against her sweaty side.

"So, here I am, Mum. Now what?" Bronte whispered.

ACKNOWLEDGMENTS

I am sure no book would be written without support from many. In my case, I would like to thank my long time friend, Hilary, who has encouraged and supported me from the first tentative suggestion, sharing with her my dream of writing a book, to its realisation.

Thanks to my incredible editors, Anna and Lauren at CreativeINK, your help and enthusiasm has been both invaluable and much appreciated. Lana Pecherczyk, your efficiency and talent in preparing gorgeous covers is amazing – thank you from the bottom of my heart.

To my special friends and family, thank you for your love and for believing in me. To you, dear readers, thank you for choosing to join me in Grace's story, the first in the Tullagulla series.

Last but by no mean least, thank you to Roger, my husband, for the never-ending hours of support and listening to me read aloud, for all your suggestions, constructive critique and delicious dinners. I could not have done this without you.

ABOUT THE AUTHOR

Born and raised in New Zealand, the highlight of Heather's childhood was the family sheep and cattle farm just north of Auckland. With reading and writing a big part of family life, she dreamed of becoming a writer, however work, travel and raising a family consumed many years after she settled in Queensland with her Australian husband. Her love and knowledge of farming life was strengthened by life on the land in Queensland's Darling Downs. Now retired and living near Toowoomba with her husband, dogs and chooks, Heather is finally able to fulfil her dream of writing. When not busy at her desk, Heather is in their large garden, minding her grandchildren, or bush walking and exploring the vast beauty of Australia and New Zealand.

Find out more at: www.heatherreyburn.com